McConnel

by

David Lemon

SOCCIONES

ISBN: 9781983207440

Cover design & formatting by Socciones Editoria Digitale
www.socciones.co.uk

Dedication

This one is for Deborah Taylor who has shown incredible emotional
strength and resilience over the past few years.

I am proud of you Babe.

For

Beth xx

Nothing to do with
Africa but
Hope you enjoy
it.

JLNS 2022.

Acknowledgements

My thanks are due to Shelagh Brown who picked me up when I was down and gave me back the urge to write. She also spent hours poring over the manuscript and correcting my sometimes abominable punctuation. Without her assistance and encouragement, McConnel would have remained a forgotten figment of my imagination.

PROLOGUE

Hilary Bedwell wrinkled her nose in distaste as they drew up behind the house in the clearing. Around her, skeletal trees seemed to creak in early morning mist and overnight rain dripped eerily off the cottage eaves.

"What is this place?" She enquired of her companion.

"It's where the local crusties hang out, Sarge," PC Jeff Maddox frowned in obvious irritation. "In another age, I suppose you would have called it a commune. Now it is just a place where a load of scumbags live together and cause trouble – know what I mean?"

"Crusties?" Hilary queried with a small smile.

"Yeah – crusties; we call 'em that because they never bloody well wash, so the dirt is encrusted on their skins – know what I mean? There are four or five families living here at the minute and they really are a waste of oxygen, I can tell you. I don't suppose you can call them New Age Travellers, but they all seem to have dropped out of society for one reason or another. They spend their useless lives stoned out of their tiny minds and nicking whatever isn't tied down – know what I mean?"

"I suppose they fancy themselves as gypsies, do they? We had some genuine gypsies at my last nick, but they were actually quite useful. We had to move them on eventually though because local folk were starting to complain. Are this lot part of that fraternity or whatever it is?"

"Nah Sarge," Maddox sounded unimpressed. "We've had gypsies and tinkers in the area before, but this lot are nothing like that. At least the real didikois can do the odd job or two when they aren't thieving – know what I mean? These just steal the air we breathe and do fuck all."

"Do they give us any actual trouble?" The tall blonde sergeant looked around her with a little more interest and Maddox frowned.

"The local farmers occasionally come in with complaints about their dogs running wild, but they aren't too bad for scrotes, I suppose," he admitted grudgingly. "They are all dirty as hell and a pain in the arse, but we don't have too much to do with them."

The engine of the big police car was still ticking over and Maddox switched it off abruptly. In the sudden silence, a magpie chattered hysterically and Hilary shivered as she climbed from the car.

The house was a battered little cottage made from crumbling, grey Cotswold stone. A number of slates were missing from the roof and the place looked run down and decrepit in the early morning light. A few stray rays of sunshine breaking through the forest mist only served to light up a couple of cracked and broken windows and the building looked as though it was being held together by the ivy that covered the entire front wall. There was no sign of life from inside and Hilary looked a little bleakly at the other dwellings.

These consisted of two wooden prefabs, a patched tepee on a strip of muddy grass and an old red bus with torn curtains across the windows. Even in the fresh morning air, an atmosphere of unwashed decay hung over the clearing. The wet ground had been churned into mud and two pied crows ignored the police officers as they hopped disinterestedly in their search for titbits. Watching them, Hilary sourly admired their optimism. The desolate surroundings did not seem to offer much in the way of pickings, even for crows.

A magpie cackled somewhere in the woods and a line of discoloured nappies fluttered noisily from a line of baling twine, strung between the bus and a nearby ash tree. A shaggy Alsatian dog looked up dispiritedly from a length of rope attached to the front bumper of the bus, but – apart from the crows – it was the only visible sign of life. Hilary and her companion ignored the big animal.

A movement beneath the bus caught the young sergeant's eye and she dropped on to her haunches to see a grimy toddler playing in thick mud between the rear wheels of the bus. Seeming to feel the policewoman's gaze, the child looked up at the interlopers without curiosity, while stirring dribble from its nose with a dirt-encrusted finger.

Hilary shuddered, a wave of revulsion coming over her at the obvious squalor with which she was surrounded.

"How can they live like this?" She muttered to her companion. "I'll bet that even the dog is used to better things."

Jeff Maddox grinned.

"What's the matter, Sarge? This sort of scene not quite what you're used to then?"

There was a hint of sarcasm in his tone and Hilary bridled instinctively. As a new sergeant to the station – and a female at that – she knew that she was very much on trial with older men like Maddox and he would be keen to exploit any apparent weaknesses.

"I can cope, PC Maddox," she snapped. "I just hate to see kids brought up in these sorts of surroundings. What chance do they have of making a life for themselves when their early years are spent like this?"

The infant seemed aware that it was the subject under discussion. Watching the two officers through soulful blue eyes, he or she (it was difficult to tell) wore only a filthy tee shirt, but did not seem to notice the early morning chill. Crawling through the mud toward the tethered dog, it peered out into the wan sunshine and the animal whined happily as it nuzzled beneath the toddler's flimsy garment.

Maddox laughed sardonically.

"I wouldn't worry too much about that one if I were you, Sarge. Give it a year or three and it will be an expert in all aspects of petty villainy – know what I mean? These places serve up bloody good apprenticeships in crime, I can tell you."

Gesturing loosely at the general untidiness of their surroundings, he moved purposefully toward the wide-eyed infant. At his approach, the child hooked one hand into the dog's fur and pulled itself laboriously to its feet from where it watched the advance of the big policeman.

"We are the police," Maddox announced unnecessarily, and the infant's expression did not alter. "We want to speak to your father – know what I mean? Where is he?"

The child continued stirring the snot on its face and the dog whined hungrily. Shaking his head in angry frustration, PC Maddox took another heavy step forward.

"Piss off, Copper."

The uncouth dismissal was uttered in clear, piping tones and brought Jeff Maddox to an incredulous halt. Five paces behind him, Hilary struggled to hide her smile at the expression on the big man's face.

"What did you say?" He demanded angrily, big hands suddenly balled into fists at his side.

"She said, 'piss off,' so why don't you do just that?"

The quietly spoken words made Hilary look up abruptly, to see a thin, bearded man descending from the bus. He presented a somewhat eccentric appearance in striped pyjamas and a woollen bobble hat of faded green. The pyjamas were far too small for his rangy frame and bony wrists protruded from the sleeves. His eyes were a strange, translucent green and as he looked at Hilary and her companion, they were decidedly hostile.

"Are you in charge here?"

Hilary spoke in measured tones, studying the man as she did so.

Although he was thin, his shoulders were broad, and he moved with the easy suppleness of an athlete. Lank brown hair tumbled around his neck and his beard was full and uncombed. He wore a silver ring in one ear and a string of brightly coloured beads around his neck. His feet were bare, and Hilary noticed with disgust that his toenails had not been cut for some time. Each nail was thickly ingrained with black grime and although she couldn't see them, she had no doubt that his fingernails were the same.

Older than most of the travelling fraternity, he must have been in his early thirties and returned her appraisal with studied insolence.

"What if I am?"

He spoke quietly, and his tone was neutral, but there was an underlying note of antagonism that was unmistakable.

Hilary was not to be put off. Jeff Maddox was watching her and she knew that her handling of the situation would be thoroughly discussed and analysed among her colleagues back at the station. Most of them would be keen to find some chink in her personal armour that they could exploit in times to come.

"You'll do for the moment," she told the bearded one. "What is your name?"

"Who is asking and why should I tell you anyway?" He countered and for a moment, Hilary hesitated.

"I am Sergeant Bedwell from the local police station." She made an effort to keep her voice polite and friendly. "We are looking for a young girl who has gone missing and we…"

"So you immediately came out here to check us out," he finished for her and this time, his tone was angrily sarcastic. "Why is it you people always pick on us when anything goes wrong?"

"We are hardly 'picking on you.'" Hilary told him severely. "The girl is only thirteen and we are checking out every possible avenue."

He smiled unexpectedly, and his eyes suddenly twinkled at her, their colour changing to a deep, limpid green that brought a tingle to her spine. In spite of her aversion to his type and the gravity of the situation, Hilary couldn't help wondering what the man would look like in decent clothes and without the tangle of hair around his face.

"Sorry Sergeant," he said mildly. "We live a peaceful life out here on the Beacon, but we do get fed up when you people keep hounding us."

"You are obviously new here," he went on conversationally, "but your tame gorilla is a frequent visitor. If a car is nicked in town, then it has to be up on the Beacon. If there is a fight among local yobs, then someone from the Beacon has to be involved."

"He knows damned well that we would not keep a missing person here, but because we don't conform to what he feels is normal, he keeps hassling us, just to show what a hell of a fine fellow he is."

The words were spoken quietly and without undue self-pity, but Hilary sensed the underlying bitterness that provoked them. Then, the man smiled again and she couldn't help noticing that his voice was beautifully modulated and held no trace of an accent. Whoever he was, this man did not sound or act at all like the average hippy or New Age Traveller.

Certainly none that Hilary Bedwell had come across.

Jeff Maddox moved truculently towards him.

"Don't try and be clever, Scumbag," the big policeman snarled. "It's too early in the morning for smart arses – know what I mean?"

The bearded one ignored him. His green eyes remained on Hilary's face and she shifted uncomfortably at the derision in their depths.

"I will deal with it, PC Maddox," she said severely, then turned her attention back to the pyjama clad hippie.

"I asked for your name," she said mildly. "I've told you who we are and why we are here. Now I would like to know who I am talking to."

Teeth gleamed white within the recesses of the beard and the twinkle in those disturbing green eyes grew more pronounced.

"Call me McConnel."

"What McConnel? You must have another name."

He shook his head a little wearily.

"Just McConnel, Sergeant. We don't bother with additional names in our society. We have no need for them."

The grimy toddler interrupted the proceedings by hurling a piece of wet mud at the police officers. McConnel's eyes flickered and Hilary automatically turned toward the child. So did Maddox and as he did so, the big dog snarled and lunged forward to nip him in the right calf. Swearing violently, the policeman raised a beefy fist and turned on the animal. In a flash, the atmosphere changed.

McConnel's eyes paled until they were almost white, and his face became cold and angry. Without seeming to hurry, he moved with astonishing speed, stepping past Hilary and gripping the big policeman's upraised arm in one hand. Maddox' face darkened in his anger, but he was unable to resist the pressure of the smaller man's hand.

"You touch that dog, Copper and I will tear you apart, uniform or no ruddy uniform."

The words were spoken very softly, but they held infinite menace, and for a moment nobody moved. Hilary immediately reasserted her authority.

"Leave the animal alone, PC Maddox," she ordered peremptorily, then turned angrily on the young man.

"Mr McConnel, or whatever your name is, I have come here to look for a missing girl. You are obstructing me and I will not stand for that, whatever the provocation."

Drawing the official photograph from her tunic pocket, Hilary moved toward the man, still standing beside PC Maddox. Handing him the print, she was uncomfortably aware of the rich smell, emanating from his body. It was obviously some time since he had washed, but the smell was overpoweringly male and in spite of her automatic disgust, Hilary felt a strange tingling in the pit of her stomach. The green eyes were warm again and regarded her with obvious amusement. She wondered whether he knew what she was feeling, and the thought made her flush with embarrassment.

"That is the girl," she struggled to cover her confusion with brisk efficiency. "Her name is Alison Mayberry and she disappeared the day before yesterday. Her parents think she might have joined the travelling fraternity, which is why we came up here."

"We are not travellers," he told her softly. "We have our own alternative society and don't want to be confused with any other life group."

He gestured around him and Hilary was suddenly aware that others had appeared on the scene and were watching the curious confrontation.

Two scruffy individuals slouched in the back doorway of the cottage, a tousled female head poked from the tepee and others stood outside the wooden dwellings. In the bus behind McConnel, a faded blonde woman in her early twenties, held a baby to her breast and regarded the police officers with hostile eyes.

"What do they want, McConnel?"

The blonde snapped the question, but he waved her away. Among his own kind, he had a definite air of authority and was obviously the natural leader of the group.

"Worry not, Ellie Dear," he advised airily. "Yet again, the forces of law and order seem to think we can help them, but I will sort it out."

He turned his attention back to Hilary.

"Why don't you let your gorilla have a good look around, Sergeant? None of us have anything to hide and he looks the sort to get a thrill out of seeing half-dressed females."

He glanced contemptuously at Jeff Maddox and Hilary felt the big policeman stiffen indignantly. She turned towards him before he could react violently to the studied insolence of the words.

"Have a quick look through, PC Maddox," she told him brusquely. "There is no need to disturb anyone, but we'll just make absolutely sure that young Alison is not here, before leaving these people in peace."

Scowling with sorely affronted anger, PC Jeff Maddox stood for a long moment in front of the man called McConnel. He was rubbing his wrist where the hippie had grabbed it and Hilary was surprised to see the raw, red weal that had sprung up from the pressure of the bearded man's fingers.

"You're too clever for your own good, Arsehole," Maddox grated roughly. "My turn will come and when it does, I'm really going to enjoy it – know what I mean?"

"PC Maddox," Hilary interrupted firmly. "Get on with it please and let's leave your private feuds aside for another time."

Maddox glared back at her and she did not miss the naked hostility in the look. Without another word, he pushed past the pyjama-clad man and moved into the bus. Hilary remained standing outside, with McConnel, a flash of insolent colour in front of her. The other hippies stood or sat stolidly around the little clearing and their hostile eyes followed Jeff Maddox' progress.

Nobody said a word.

"Why is this place known as 'The Beacon?'"

Hilary ventured the question in an effort to break the suddenly oppressive silence.

McConnel smiled.

"It is actually the hill behind us that has the survey beacon." He waved one arm expansively around him. "The house is officially, 'Beacon Cottage' and we call ourselves the Beacon Community, but over the past few months, we seem to have become 'The Beacon' ourselves."

His explanation was interrupted by the return of Jeff Maddox, still nursing his wrist and still looking murderous. The burly constable shrugged at Hilary.

"Nothing here, Sarge. Wherever the little bitch might be, these crusties haven't got her."

Behind him, the dog growled deep in its chest and he shifted uneasily away from the big animal. McConnel looked amused, but nobody else reacted in any way.

"Okay, let's move on then," Hilary decided before turning back to the hippie leader.

"I am sorry to have bothered you, Mr McConnel," she told him. "We'll leave you to get on with your day."

"Till the next time," McConnel commented sourly. "No doubt something else will crop up and your immediate reaction will be to check us out again."

Hilary opened her mouth to protest, but Maddox took her arm.

"Come on, Sarge," he gritted. "This scrote is just trying to wind you up."

Hilary allowed herself to be guided back to the car and strapped herself in while Maddox slid into the driving seat. As she eased the seat belt across her bosom, McConnel called to her across the clearing.

"Sergeant Bedwell?"

She turned her face towards him.

"Yes, what is it?"

He smiled again, and she couldn't help marvelling at how attractive the gesture made him look. The eyes that had been so cold and hard when he spoke to Maddox, now softened to the consistency of warm forest pools.

"If you are ever at a loose end, why don't you drop in for a cup of tea and a chat? We're not as bad as we are painted, you know. I am sure you will find yourself pleasantly surprised at the welcome we lay on for visitors."

"I might even take you up on that, McConnel."

Before she could say more, Maddox had the car moving and he drove directly toward the bearded hippie. McConnel made no effort to move out of the way and his eyes were cold again and filled with contempt as the white bonnet passed within millimetres of his flapping pyjama jacket.

Hilary reacted angrily.

"Don't be a bloody fool, PC Maddox," she snapped. "What has that man done to you except make you look a prat? There is no point in deliberately antagonising these people and if you had hit him, we would both be in serious trouble."

The big constable made no reply, but his lips were a tight slash across his face and his eyes were sullen. They returned to the police station in a tense and uncomfortable silence.

The man, known only as McConnel, watched the vehicle move off with a thoughtful expression on his features. The blonde watched him closely from the door of the bus and the toddler went back to stirring the dribbles from its nose.

CHAPTER ONE

"You will need to include her immediate impressions at the scene, Mark."

The speaker was Hilary Bedwell and she was studying a statement form, produced for her inspection by the young constable standing attentively beside her chair. Other papers and plans from a thick accident file were placed haphazardly about the surface of her desk and Hilary was trying hard to concentrate. As the early turn relief sergeant, she had intended to spend little time on paperwork, but the youngster had made a complete mess of his initial enquiries and she knew that sorting it all out would probably take up much of the morning.

A knock on the door made her frown in annoyance.

"What is it?" She demanded, as a civilian reception clerk put her head around the door. "I am terribly busy, Sheila. Can't it wait?"

"I've got a very smelly hippy type asking for you at the front desk, Sarge."

Still studying the statement form, Hilary sucked absently on her pen.

"What does he want?"

The girl shrugged.

"I don't know. He refused to tell me. Just said he wanted you and nobody else would do."

"Oh damn!" Hilary sighed. "I really do not have time for idle chatter right now. Go back and find out exactly what he wants please Sheila. If he really won't see anyone else, have him come back in an hour."

"Okay Sarge."

The girl turned to go and as she reached the door, Hilary glanced up again, a sudden thought making her hesitate.

"Did this bloke say who he was, Sheila?"

The girl frowned.

"He called himself McDonald or O Connel, Sarge. He wouldn't tell me any more than that."

Hilary caught her breath. It was a week since she and Jeff Maddox had visited the little community on Swanwick Beacon. A week since she had seen the scruffy character with the pyjamas and compelling eyes. Her visit to the beacon had been a fleeting one and should have been quickly forgotten in the turmoil of her everyday life, yet in the week since she had seen him, she had thought about McConnel far more often than was strictly proper. His air of natural authority and his dignified manner had made a strong impression on her and she found him difficult to get out of her mind.

Even as she stood up from the desk, she had a sudden memory of the bearded man's cold anger when Jeff Maddox had moved to hit the dog and she felt an involuntary shiver as she remembered his silent attack on the burly officer. Back at the police station, Maddox had displayed the injury to his wrist – a livid weal that even then was turning a deep purple.

"That skinny little arsehole doesn't know his own strength," the aggrieved constable had told his wondering colleagues. "I'll get my own back though and he will be sorry that he ever set eyes on me – know what I mean?"

Now the same 'skinny little arsehole' wanted to see her and in spite of her busy schedule, Hilary felt a sudden lift to her spirits. Dirty, scruffy and feckless McConnel might be, but he had a presence about him that was terribly intriguing.

Hilary had dealt with hippies or 'new age travellers' as they now called themselves on many occasions. In general, she had found them to be a shiftless lot, continually on the move and always looking for a hand out or an easy chance. Those she had come up against seemed to care little for the feelings of others, but were quick to complain when they felt in any way put upon themselves. Hilary had even known them produce a tame lawyer when the occasion demanded it and they were strong and vociferous on the subject of human rights – but only when it was their own rights that were threatened.

McConnel was doubtless as idle and useless as the rest, but he certainly had something about him that bore further looking into. Shaking her head and sighing with feigned impatience, Sergeant Hilary Bedwell turned to her young subordinate.

"Give me five minutes please, Mark. I have an idea what this chap wants and once it is sorted out, we will get back to your accident file, I promise."

Gathering up his scattered papers, the young constable bundled them into the file and made for the report room, while his sergeant unconsciously straightened her tunic and glanced in a wall mirror in preparation for her meeting with the man known only as McConnel.

***

Although he was fully dressed, McConnel's appearance was every bit as bizarre as it had been at their first meeting.

He wore an old duffel coat that might once have been brown and was enlivened with clumsy repair work in a variety of hues. Beneath the coat was a grimy work shirt with a badly frayed collar, torn and faded jeans and heavy brown boots with laces made from orange baler twine. On his unkempt head, the same woollen bobble hat perched precariously and McConnel's ensemble was enlivened by a bright red scarf and a string of coloured beads around his neck.

At Hilary's appearance, he straightened from where he was slouching against one wall and smiled a welcome. Once again, the trim police sergeant couldn't help noticing how the gesture lit up his face.

"What do you want?" She demanded, her gruff manner serving only to hide the ambivalence of her feelings towards her unkempt visitor.

"Is that any way to greet an old friend?" He grinned disarmingly. "I wanted only to speak with you, Sergeant Bedwell."

"How did you know my name?"

"You told me. Remember?" He spread his hands wide in front of him and she grudgingly admitted that she did. "I was passing by and thought I would drop in with a snippet or two of information that might prove useful in your work."

Hilary hesitated. Any police officer new to a district needs to build up a network of informers, yet this man's sheer presence made her feel distinctly uneasy. Surely he would never make a snout? Stifling her momentary misgivings, she moved to one side of the counter and raised a wooden flap, allowing him access to the reception area.

"Okay McConnel, come on in, but I'm warning you, this had better be good. I am a very busy woman, you know."

Once again white teeth flashed within the beard and the green eyes twinkled. Hilary couldn't help smiling back, then led the way to her office.

As they moved past a bare concrete staircase, she hesitated, then – on a whim she could never after explain – turned back to her companion.

"Do you fancy a cup of tea?"

"Ever the gracious hostess," he murmured the words into his beard and nodded his head. She led him up four flights of stairs to the canteen on the top floor and when they arrived, she was not really surprised to discover that McConnel did not seem in any way out of breath. Most visitors to the canteen who did not take the lift were left in a state of imminent collapse, particularly when they were in the company of the super fit Sergeant Bedwell.

The canteen was a big, spacious room, all Formica surfaces and silver-plated tableware, with wide windows looking out on the town and a view of distant hills. When they arrived, the place was empty, apart from a serving lady and three uniformed officers playing cards at a corner table. One of the card players was PC Maddox and his mouth fell open when he saw Hilary's companion.

"Well, well, well – look what the cat's brought in," he muttered to his companions. "Our lovely skipper is really scraping the barrel this time – know what I mean?"

A younger man laughed coarsely and made no attempt to conceal his mirth.

"Some of those fancy birds like a bit of rough, Jeff," he grinned. "Must turn 'em on somehow I reckon."

Hilary tensed, and blood suffused her cheeks, but she kept a smile on her face and showed her companion to a table, well away from the one occupied by Maddox and his cronies.

"What'll you have – tea?" She asked him shortly and at his nod, walked up to the long counter where she gave her order to the serving lady.

Alone at the table McConnel smiled into his neckerchief and if he was in any way embarrassed at being the focus for every eye in the room, he gave no sign of it.

Moments later, Hilary Bedwell returned with two mugs of tea and put one of them down in front of him.

"I am sure you must be hungry, so I've ordered a couple of breakfasts as well," she told him. "Now, tell me what you are after."

Although she spoke quietly, the silence in the room was such that her words seemed to echo around the walls and she was immediately aware of it.

Turning in her seat, she glared at Jeff Maddox and his companions, who sat watching her and McConnel with undisguised curiosity.

"While I don't doubt that you have my welfare very much to heart, Gentlemen," she spoke with heavy sarcasm, "this is a private conversation and I would appreciate it remaining so."

"I know what you mean, Sarge," Maddox called across the room. "There are matters that should always remain secret between men and women, don't you think? We were a little worried though. A lonely police canteen is no place for a girl on her own – know what I mean? You never know what sort of low life you might meet up with."

The sally brought open grins from his companions, but a moment later, the three men packed their cards away and took their dirty dishes up to the counter before making a noisy exit from the room.

McConnel watched them go with a broad grin.

"That won't have done your reputation too much good, Sergeant B," he commented mildly. "Give it half an hour and every copper in the county will know that you were breakfasting with a bad lot. And in the police canteen too."

Hilary laughed flatly but there was no humour in the sound.

"They can mind their own business then, McConnel, can't they? I am not going to let Jeff Maddox or anyone else tell me what I can or cannot do."

"Maddox was the big one? The bloke you brought out to our place last week?"

She nodded grimly, and he frowned.

"Be careful there, Sergeant Bedwell. That is the second time you have cut him down in front of me and he won't like either of us for that."

"Too bad," she said flatly and looked hard at McConnel over the rim of her mug.

"Right then McConnel, that is enough about my problems. Why were you so keen to see me?"

Before he could speak, they were interrupted by a call from the serving lady and Hilary left the table again to collect breakfast for them both. McConnel's eyes widened at the size of the repast placed in front of him.

Bacon, two fried eggs, fried bread, sausage, mushrooms and tomato – all served in lavish proportions. He glanced somewhat quizzically at the police sergeant.

"An unexpected treat, Sergeant Bedwell. Do I look so much in need of feeding up then?"

Hilary smiled a trifle uncomfortably.

"It was time for my breakfast anyway, so we might as well eat together while you tell me what you want."

In truth, Hilary was a little bewildered by her own actions. Not normally a social person, she preferred to eat alone when she could, yet here she was, sitting down to breakfast with a complete stranger and a man whose appearance alone should have filled her with disgust. It did not make sense, but she justified the idiosyncrasy by telling herself that it was merely an assertion of her own independence. Jeff Maddox and the other PCs were so obviously disapproving that she was determined not to let them dictate her actions.

Even to herself, the justification was not entirely convincing and Hilary felt suddenly embarrassed by the situation in which she found herself. She was acting out of character and could not have said why. McConnel seemed to have bewitched her and she was not sure whether she enjoyed it or not. Surreptitiously, she studied her strange companion.

In spite of his bizarre appearance, the young man on the opposite side of the table possessed an obvious dignity that she found fascinating. His soft tones were almost cultured and he seemed far more intelligent than most of her companions in the police service. He spoke wittily on a variety of subjects and something within him struck a deep personal chord with her own feelings. Hilary even admitted somewhat wryly to herself that in a strangely compelling way, she even found him attractive.

But it was an uncomfortable thought and she brusquely pushed it aside. Hilary Bedwell was an ambitious and capable police officer, very much on the way up. She came from a good, solid background and her future in the service seemed assured. The man at the table with her was a drop out, one of the casualties of modern living and very much part of Society's dregs. In normal circumstances, she wouldn't be seen dead talking with him, let alone enjoying a meal in his company.

The deep green eyes were studying her with as much care as she was paying to him.

"A penny for them, Sergeant,," he spoke softly, and she felt herself colouring involuntarily.

"I was just marvelling at what a strange pair we make," she admitted ruefully and he laughed aloud, throwing his head back, the rank locks spilling messily from beneath his woollen cap.

"Ah yes," he mused when he had recovered his breath. "'Graduate police sergeant forsakes promising career to follow the hippy trail.' What a story that would make."

"How did you know I was a graduate?" She spoke without looking at him, concentrating on her bacon and eggs. For his part, he ate with enormous gusto, wolfing down the food and wiping up excess egg yolk with his toast. There was nothing even remotely decorous about his eating. It was merely the action of a hungry animal filling its belly and she struggled to keep her eyes off his blackened fingernails. Although she felt herself repelled by his lack of table manners, she couldn't help but enjoy his whole-hearted enthusiasm for the food.

"I made it my business to find out," he grinned impudently around a mouthful of toast. "It wasn't too difficult. You are quite a famous character in this area, you know. Twenty-six years old and unmarried – although with your looks that is surely a crime! Daughter of a leading clergyman," it was as though he was reading from a dossier, "educated at Rendlecombe Ladies College and Oxford, where you read classical languages. Then, for some reason that nobody will ever understand, you attested into the local constabulary as a beat bobby.

'Of course, you were never destined to stay in that lowly position for long. In your examination for promotion to sergeant, you came third in the entire country and were immediately whipped off to join the Special Course at Bramshill Police College. Now you are working out your mandatory year as a uniformed sergeant, but from here on, your promotions will be rapid. Provided you stay out of trouble, you should end up as chief constable of some obscure police force where – as a woman – you can't do too much damage to the Establishment.

'That is of course if you don't get married, take to drink or," his eyes twinkled extravagantly, "forsake the path of respectability and join the New Age community."

Snorting derisively into her tea, she could not help expressing her amazement.

17

"How on earth did you discover all that?"

"The forces of law and order are not the only ones with sources of information, Sergeant Bedwell,." He admonished primly. "In my world too, we have a vast network of useful contacts and with a little effort can find out anything at all."

Their plates were empty, and he accepted her offer of another mug of tea. For Hilary, it was an opportunity to collect her thoughts. In spite of his airy disclaimers, this uncouth individual had obviously gone to a great deal of trouble to discover all that he could about her. But why should he do that and how had he managed it? Most of the information he had come out with should not have been available to the general public, let alone the hippy community. Shaking her head in bemusement, she returned to the table.

"I won't ask any more about your sources, McConnel," she told him quietly. "But why did you bother? An ordinary police officer can surely be no more than a passing irritation to you and your kind."

Scratching furiously at his beard, he frowned at her and there was a look of hurt in the green eyes.

"I don't think I like that, Sergeant. Who or what are 'my kind'? Just because I do not conform with what Society expects of me, does that put me into some special category? I know I don't dress very well," the twinkle was back in his eyes and she laughed, "but that is surely my choice to make. Your lot, and most of the general public usually class me as a traveller, but I work, I pay my taxes and belong to a settled community. The trouble is that you lump us all together on appearance, even though most of us are nothing like the louts you see on the television news from time to time.

'Yet even the New Age Travellers are a society in their own right and you would be surprised at some of the folk who have taken to life on the road.

'As to why I bothered – well, I sensed a strange sort of empathy between us when you came up to the Beacon. You seemed much more sympathetic and understanding than the average plod and I was intrigued.

'Besides, you are far too pretty and far too sensitive to be a copper."

Once again, Hilary felt herself colouring and tried to fight it back. Noticing her confusion, he smiled quietly – which only made matters worse.

"So," he went on, "I made it my business to find out what I could about you. My lot," he invested the words with heavy sarcasm, "don't normally get on too well with the Old Bill, and I would like to see that change. After all,

I – and my type of course – can be of enormous use to you and vice versa. Why then, can't we be friendlier towards each other?"

He waved his mug at her and for once in her life, Hilary Bedwell – graduate in classical languages and would be police commissioner – found herself totally lost for words. She stared in silent amazement at McConnel, then the moment was broken by the noisy arrival of two young constables, in for a late breakfast. They sobered as they took in the sight of their sergeant and her strange companion, then they moved across to the service counter and Hilary stood up.

"To some extent, I agree with you, McConnel. This world is big enough for all sorts of people to co-exist in harmony. There should be no reason at all why people should not drop out and do their own thing in whatever way they want to. All too often though, they do it at the expense of others and that is when the friction starts. I don't think there is much that either of us can do about that.

'Now I have work to do, so I'll show you out before my prospects for further promotion are ruined forever."

Grinning through his beard, McConnel followed her meekly out of the canteen. As she showed him through the reception area, he paused and turned towards her. Hilary was suddenly aware of the overwhelming maleness of him and she couldn't help a sudden sharp sense of self-disgust at the feeling.

"I promised you information," he said slowly, his limpid eyes seeming to stare right into her soul. "May I suggest that you pay a visit to a chap called Abie Whitehead who lives at number eighteen in Lennox Street. You might be pleasantly surprised at what you find in his house."

With that, he was gone. Like a shadow in the night, one moment he was there and the next he was not, leaving Hilary to shake her head at the abruptness of his departure. In a distinctly thoughtful frame of mind, she returned to her office where she sat for a long time, staring into space and musing on the strange encounter. Whatever else he might be, the man who called himself McConnel certainly had a way about him. His information was probably good too and she jotted down the name and address he had given her.

However, that could wait. First, she had to find out about the man himself. Where did he come from? What was his background? Why was he with those dreadful hippies? Was he married?

At the thought, she frowned. Always totally honest with herself, Hilary was surprised to find that she did not want him to be married, even though it was nothing to do with her. With a sense of deep self-revulsion, she remembered the slatternly, blonde girl on the steps of the bus and felt her insides turn over at the picture of McConnel and the girl together.

Laughing hollowly at her own idiocy, Sergeant Hilary Bedwell picked up the telephone and dialled the number of the constables' report room.

"PC Clements," she said shortly when her call was answered. "Sorry for the delay, but I'm ready for you now. Bring that accident file back and let's sort it out once and for all."

Without more ado, Hilary Bedwell got back to work, but for the rest of that morning, she found it very difficult to concentrate.

CHAPTER TWO

Wood smoke hung over the clearing and flickering firelight accented the shadows. Apart from the chortle of a distant pheasant, the evening air was quiet and McConnel felt entirely at peace.

Sitting on an old car seat, the bearded hippy stared contentedly into the flames as he smoked. The loaded cigarette was passed on to his companion and the sweetly acrid smell of marijuana drifted through the silence. This was the best time of the day. The woodland air was still and an atmosphere of tranquillity permeated the darkness. Below him, the lights of the town were spread out in spectacular profusion and McConnel felt a sudden sense of enormous sympathy for the people down there. They were trapped in their tiny houses like so many battery chickens, nothing but traffic sounds and the doubtful joys of television to entertain them. He felt a sense of enormous relief that he had escaped a similar fate and could now live his life exactly as he wanted to live it.

Swanwick Beacon was a noted beauty spot and a favourite place for picnickers and courting couples. Set in the middle of rolling Cotswold farm land, the beacon itself offered panoramic views of patched fields where sheep grazed in profusion, as well as the darker shadows of beech woods and the occasional rustic farm house with its attendant outbuildings. Way out to the East, the outskirts of the town could be seen, buildings and streets appearing almost toy like in the distance.

It was two years since McConnel and Ellie had moved in to the little encampment behind the cottage and they had been happy years. Between them, they ran a market stall in the town, where on three days a week, McConnel sold colourful jewellery made from semi-precious stones. The gems themselves were obtained from as far afield as India, Sri Lanka and Zimbabwe, while Ellie's deft fingers fashioned them into necklaces, bracelets, earrings and brooches. Their wares had proved popular in the community and although they did not make much money from the enterprise, it was enough to keep them in food and the little bit of dope that they used. It was a good life and McConnel was happy. At least, he had been happy until Hilary Bedwell had appeared on the scene.

Since the blonde police sergeant had visited their home, McConnel had been restless and dissatisfied with his lot. Her pretty, very English looks had awakened long dormant feelings inside him that left him uncomfortable and longing for something different. There could never be any prospect of a future with the girl, but she preyed on his mind and even invaded his dreams while he was asleep. It was three weeks since he had first seen her, but in that time, McConnel had become moody, withdrawn and irritable. He knew it too, but there seemed to be little he could do about it.

An insomniac pigeon hooted monotonously in the trees behind him, but it was the only sound to disturb the peace of the moment. Yet for all the apparent tranquillity, McConnel felt tense and uncomfortable. Kicking at a log in the fire, he sighed deeply and the girl glanced across at him.

"What did that mean, McConnel?" She demanded abruptly and her voice was shrill.

"What?"

He turned to face her and the pupils of his eyes were dilated from the effects of the hash.

"That sigh like. Aren't we good enough for you any more then? Are you missin' your 'ome comforts all of a sudden or are you thinkin' of that fuzz bitch again?"

He smiled gently at her through the darkness and his voice was soothing when he spoke again.

"Neither, my dear Ellie. I was merely enjoying the peace and quiet, so if I sighed, it was a sigh of pure contentment. This is surely what life is all about."

He gestured vaguely about him with a wide sweep of his arm.

"Look around you, Girl. See the trees – so tall, so old and so wise in their antiquity. See the shadows and let them colour your dreams. While you are about it, see the people in the houses down there and pity them for the drabness of their lives. Pity those who have no dreams to push them along and pity folk like poor Sergeant Bedwell who you dislike so much."

For a long moment, Ellie was silent then she turned on him again.

"You do talk a lot of bollocks, McConnel. I reckon you do it cos you know you can confuse me with your fancy words an' all. I don' like your Sergeant Bedwell for what she is, that's all. She is a pig, just like the rest of the pigs an' she'd send either of us down the road without even thinking about it. I dunno what you see in 'er, I really don't."

"Nothing, my lovely Ellie; nothing at all. As you say, she is a pig, but that doesn't stop me from feeling sorry for the lass. Whether you like her or not, she is a victim of her circumstances and upbringing, just like so many others."

Pausing for a moment, he took another deep drag from the reefer and when he spoke again, his voice was softer, his tone almost absent as though his mind was far away.

"Just as I was before I broke away from it all."

Ellie stood up abruptly, her lips pursed and her eyes angry in spite of the dope. With little fists balled on her hips, she faced the lounging McConnel.

"It is more than that, McConnel and you know it," He winced at the stridency of her tone. "You haven't been the same since those coppers came here after that stupid girl and I know you went in to see your precious sergeant at the nick in town. You even talk about her in your sleep nowadays."

He smiled lazily and his teeth shone in the firelight.

"Do I indeed? Well doesn't that just go to show the depths of my pity for her and her kind?"

"You and your fancy words." Ellie spat. "You don't take nothin' seriously and you always try to make me feel bad with your talk. You know I can never...."

She broke off and her eyes filled with tears.

"Oh what's the fuckin' use McConnel? If you want 'er, you 'ave 'er. I don't care."

She ran off into the darkness and McConnel watched her go, a hint of deep unhappiness in his eyes. He had no wish to hurt Ellie. She had been his woman for a long time and had borne him two fine children. She was always faithful and honest by her own lights.

She was also incurably dull.

Shaking his head in infinite weariness, McConnel had to admit to himself that Ellie was a long way from being the ideal companion. His background and hers were far removed from each other and there was little communion between them on an intellectual level. Her world revolved around her babies and she cared for nothing that was not enclosed within the sides of the old red bus. Even among the other Beacon women, Ellie was a recognised dunderhead and in his bleaker moments, McConnel often wondered why he had picked her for his companion.

Perhaps it was merely the contrast with all the others he had known in the course of a not uneventful life. A brilliantly talented mother, two sisters who had excelled at university and in government posts, then a succession of notably intellectual females who had shared his bed and his life, albeit on a strictly temporary basis.

Yet each one of those others had used him for their own ends and each one had taken a little more from his soul while adding their own marks to the composite personality that was McConnel. In truth, he had never really regretted taking up with Ellie. Her very lack of personality or sophistication seemed to soothe the torment that so often raged inside his being. Her self-centred dullness banished the demons that time and time again made his own life a misery. In a curious way, he was terribly fond of the girl. In spite of a lifelong roving eye, he hadn't looked at another female since they had quit the bonds of recognised society together and although she had little appetite for sex, she had seemed to be all that he needed from life. Her very simplicity suited his needs.

The life suited him too. It gave him time to think, dream and meditate. It gave him a deep sense of communion with the natural world and he knew that he was living as a man was supposed to live. He had his little family, his small circle of friends and the loneliness of the woods and hills to soothe his spirit. He didn't need the trappings of the twenty-first century and he didn't miss the world he had left behind with all its cruelty and horrors. In short, he knew himself for a free man who owed nothing to anybody in the world.

For McConnel it was an immensely satisfying way of life and if his intellect was rarely taxed, he saw no reason to complain. It had to be better than the frenetically horrifying existence he had left behind him.

At the thought he shrugged and took a deep pull at the cigarette. Dragging smoke into his lungs, he let the drug permeate his system and ease the sudden gnawings of anxiety in his stomach. He didn't want to worry; didn't need to worry. He had dropped out from society in order to avoid worry. If that policewoman hadn't come so precipitately into his life, all would still be well.

Sergeant Hilary Bedwell was at the root of his problems and McConnel knew it. He was far too old and cynical to believe in love at first sight or even in love for its own sake, but there had been an immediate spark of empathy between himself and the blonde police sergeant – an empathy that was pleasant, but terribly disturbing at the same time and an empathy that threatened to rock the foundations of his untrammelled existence. Nor was it all on his side. Although she had said nothing, McConnel had sensed the same feelings surfacing in Hilary Bedwell that were coursing through his own soul. He had sensed too that her bewilderment at these feelings was as great as his own.

A vixen called from deep in the woods and McConnel raised his head to listen. In the firelight, he sat completely still and his face might have been chiselled from stone. For a moment, it was the face of a hunter – a predator of the night – but once he had identified the sound, his whole body seemed to relax and he went back to his restless thoughts.

He had always been a resourceful character McConnel, but for the moment, he just did not know what to do. He and Sergeant Hilary Bedwell lived on opposite sides of an awfully high wall and there was no chance of either of them ever crossing over the top. They were each trapped in their own environment as surely as though they were chained in place. That was the way of the world and McConnel recognised that there was nothing that either of them could do about it, even had they wished to. It seemed a desperate situation and he wished momentarily that he had never set eyes on the blonde police officer.

His musing was interrupted by a shout from among the trees.

"Hey McConnel it's only us – Spike and Robbie."

Two bearded young men in patched and dirty clothing emerged from the shadows and squatted beside the fire across from McConnel. He grunted a welcome and reached across to pass over his almost finished reefer. Holding it carefully in his fingertips, the youth known as Spike took a deep drag before passing it on to Robbie who did the same before returning the smoke to McConnel. He flicked the spent end into the fire.

"Good shit that." Spike was larger than Robbie, nearly as tall as McConnel and wore thick blonde hair in a ponytail. A gold earring glimmered in the firelight.

"The best." McConnel agreed.

There was a silence while all three men gazed into the flames, then Spike spoke again.

"Picked up on a good offer today McConnel."

"Yeah?"

"Met this geezer in the Pheasant. 'E was 'andlin' a packet of bonzers and reckoned to lay 'is 'ands on some smack whenever I need it."

"Yeah?"

In spite of his non committal response, McConnel was interested. He had been wondering what else he could do to legitimately get in touch with Hilary Bedwell and this could be just what he needed. Marijuana was not regarded seriously by the police any more, but ecstasy tablets and heroin were another matter altogether.

"'E's willing to get 'old of some crack too if we want it. I've never 'ad a go at that an' all."

This last was said with a touch of wistfulness that made McConnel smile in spite of his deeper feelings. It was strange how ambitions varied in different sectors of society.

"How much was he after for this little bundle of goodies" He asked quietly and Spike shrugged in some embarrassment.

"'E gave us a price list, but we only got the ready for a few bonzers like. 'At's why we came to see you McConnel."

"Me? What can I do Fellas?"

"You're a switched on geezer, McConnel right? It's a big deal for us an' we don' want to get ripped off. We reckon we need 'bout three 'undred to build up a decent stash, but we ain't got nowhere near that yet. I'm off to the Social tomorrow like, but I don' reckon they'll cough up more than a ton, even if I'm lucky with the story I'm gonna feed 'em."

McConnel sighed into the darkness and shook his head at the two hippies.

"Why don't you guys stick to shit?" He asked wearily. "E and crack are hard going and once you're hooked, you'll need more and more of the ready to keep going. You'll both end up in the slammer again and you don't want that."

In spite of their scruffy appearances and their petty villainy, McConnel had a soft spot for the two youngsters. They meant no harm and the only people they ever injured were themselves. Both had already done time in prison and he didn't want to see them in more trouble.

"Yeah sure: I know you're right like, McConnel but we don't want this crap for ourselves like."

Shuffling closer to McConnel, he gripped him by one arm and stared intently into his face. His companion who hadn't yet said a word, nodded in vigorous agreement to what was about to be said. "But just think of the loot we can make from it right? There are all those punters out there just dyin' for the stuff and willing to pay almost anythin' we wanna ask.

'If we can just lay our 'ands on some good gear to start with, it'll set us up for future deals and the word'll soon get round. We'll be rich in no time, Man.

'Think of it, McConnel; just think of it like."

He shook the hippy leader's arm to emphasise his words and grunting in distaste, McConnel pulled away although Spike did not appear to notice the gesture.

"Word will get around alright, Spike. Around all the coppering shops in the county and then where will you be? Back in the bloody slammer before you even know what has gone wrong.

'You fellas want tea?" He went off at a tangent to give himself time to think. Both his visitors nodded enthusiastically.

"Bring us a drink please, Ellie." McConnel called into the darkness behind him and a few minutes later, the girl reappeared, her face set in sullen lines. Without a word to the visitors, she dumped a chipped and grimy mug down in front of each of them and walked back toward the shadowy bus. A baby's wail split the silence of the night and McConnel pushed a log further into the fire. Orange sparks shot up toward the filmy stars.

"Yore bird is 'ardly the most cheerful one, McConnel." Robbie broke his silence and his voice was adenoidally shrill. McConnel looked levelly across at him and his expression didn't change.

"She's alright," he said shortly, "She is worried at the moment, but she does a good job and I'm not complaining."

"What's she worried about then?" Spike put in, but McConnel shook his head.

"Leave it fellas." He advised quietly. "Her worries are mine, not yours. Let's get back to your particular problem shall we?"

Taking another loaded cigarette from his pocket, he carefully tamped the end and lit up. Taking a deep drag, he closed his eyes for a moment, then passed the joint around. The other two took their turn, and handed it back. Nobody said a word until the circle had been completed.

"I can put fifty in," McConnel said at last "I'm not prepared to go any higher and I don't want to be involved in the pushing. That is asking for grief with the filth and if you want that, then it's fine by me but leave me out of it."

Spike smiled happily and sipped at his mug of tea with a loud slurping noise.

"That'll 'elp for sure McConnel. With yore fifty and another fifty from Robbie here, we can set ourselves up with a reasonable stake like.

'I'll 'andle the dealing part see. If we keep the stuff amongst ourselves and choose the ones we sell to, there shouldn't be any trouble with the feds. I tell you Man, there's money to be made if we can only set ourselves up proper.

'Will you come with us when we see this bloke tomorrow though? I don' reckon we'll get stung if you are there."

"How will my presence help, Man? I told you, I don't want to get involved. Gear is dangerous stuff and I have enough problems on my plate as it is."

"Ah come on McConnel. With yore fancy accent and yore knowledge of these things, you can save us from being taken for a ride. You know what these big dealers are like."

McConnel thought briefly, then nodded his head in weary resignation. Someone had to look after these two or they were bound to come unstuck.

"Okay, I'll come in on it and keep an eye on you when you do the deal, but I will watch from a distance. If you run into problems with the bloke himself, I will step in, but that is all I'll do. Where the dealing and the law is concerned, you are strictly on your own. All I want is my share of any profits. Okay?"

"Kay." Spike agreed and Robbie solemnly nodded his head.

"Where and when is your meeting with this bloke set up for?

"Nine o'clock tomorra evenin' in the Pheasant."

"Okay, I'll see you there."

Shortly afterwards, Spike and Robbie slipped away through the trees. They lived with their own women in the wooden pre fabs and as he sat on by the fire, McConnel could hear someone singing quietly inside the further of the little dwellings. Half an hour after his visitors had left, he rose from the seat, kicked the smouldering logs into the fire and made his way wearily back to the bus.

Ellie was breast-feeding the baby by the light of a solitary candle and their daughter snuffled in her sleep. The dog lay across the open doorway and its hairy tail thumped briefly on the floor when it saw its master. Pausing on the threshold, McConnel took in the scene and for a moment, despair threatened to overwhelm him.

This was his home – his family – his responsibility. This sour-smelling accumulation of human and animal flotsam was all he had to show for thirty-three years of life. He had taken to the road to get away from just this sort of scene, yet here he was, saddled with Ellie and two brats – as deeply mired in convention as any city businessman with a mortgage and a pension scheme. This surely wasn't living.

Ellie's eyes were hostile as he approached.

"Why are you gettin' involved with those two now McConnel?" She demanded and he shrugged.

"It is only fifty, My Love and we could make a bit out of it if they don't get caught."

"An' if they do? You know they will drag you into it as well. You always told me you wouldn't mess wiv the 'eavy stuff. Why have you changed yore mind now?"

Irritation swept over him and he snapped at her.

"Because we need the money Ellie. The engine on this crate is dying and the kids have to be clothed. We need food and the hash that we smoke. There is another shipment of stones to pay for as well, so we need money fast. If we can make a few hundred out of this, we can then pull out and leave the lads to it. That has to be a good thing doesn't it?"

"You are a fool McConnel," she told him bitterly. "Ever since that silly bitch of a copper came here you've been acting strangely. I don't know what has got into you but that woman 'as really turned yore 'ead. You're goin' in for a big fall, just you wait and see. It'll be 'er fault too.

'Anyway, what has she got that I 'aven't?" She went on venomously. "I'm blonde too and if she is prettier than me, tha's only cos she 'asn't 'ad kids. Apart from tha', she 'as got two tits and a fanny, just the same as me. It isn't bloody fair, you know tha'?"

Wordlessly climbing into his side of the mattress on the floor, McConnel smiled wearily to himself. Although they might both be blonde, Ellie's spotty countenance put her in a totally different league to the elegantly beautiful police sergeant. Shaking his head in the darkness, he draped a quilt around his shoulders and turned his back on her.

29

"Good night," he muttered flatly and for a long moment, there was silence, broken only by the snuffling of the baby at her nipple and the gentle snores of their elder daughter.

"You are a fool McConnel," Ellie repeated quietly and he nodded silently to himself.

He was undoubtedly making a fool of himself and Ellie was right. It was all to do with Sergeant Hilary Bedwell. The blonde policewoman had addled his brain and for the first time in a good few years, McConnel didn't know what to do with himself.

CHAPTER THREE

Hilary Bedwell looked at her watch then shook her head in angry frustration. This was no time for impatience. The meeting in the pub was only due at nine and it would be a good fifteen minutes after that before any dealing would take place. Her officers were in position and there was nothing she could do to influence the course of events. She tried to concentrate on the paperwork in front of her but the brief encounter with McConnel kept coming to her mind.

The bearded hippy had approached her in the crowded shopping precinct that morning and a little to her surprise, he had shown none of his usual mocking self-confidence.

Sidling up beside her, he glanced quickly around before leaning forward to murmur in her ear. Although he appeared somewhat cleaner than usual, she was immediately aware of the sickly sweet smell that seemed to hang about his clothing. He had been smoking cannabis and the aroma would linger for hours, but she had little time to dwell on the matter.

"There's a drug deal taking place in The Speckled Pheasant tonight," he muttered tersely. "Nine o'clock in the public bar."

He was gone before she had time to respond, his woolly hat bobbing above the heads of the throng and a gap opening up in front of him wherever he passed. The likes of McConnel were not an uncommon sight in the town, but respectable citizens tended to view his kind with considerable apprehension.

Within moments he had disappeared and it was an extremely thoughtful Sergeant Bedwell who returned to the police station.

McConnel's information was likely to be good. The search of Abie Whitehead's house had yielded unexpected results. Packed carelessly into a bedroom cupboard had been a cache of electronic goods that served to clear up a number of hitherto undetected crimes in the county. Abie had supplemented his earnings as a baker's delivery man by paying after-dark visits to the houses he serviced and obviously feeling that electronics offered the best prospects for quick profits, he had concentrated on laptops, tablets, cameras and mobile phones. There was well over ten thousand pounds worth of stolen equipment in that cupboard and an initially indignant Abie had been voluble in the assistance he offered, once he realised that he had no chance of getting away with anything.

So it seemed that McConnel was genuinely keen to help and Hilary brushed aside the possible implications of reacting to his information. It was obviously personally inspired, but she was a copper and it was her duty to follow up on every possible lead. Even if McConnel was wrong and there was no drugs deal in the offing, she had to do something.

Without explaining where her information came from, she briefed Jeff Maddox and two junior constables whose faces were not likely to be known in The Speckled Pheasant. Maddox grinned in eager anticipation.

"Let's hope you're right Sarge." He seemed to have forgiven Hilary for her anger in McConnel's presence and she was quite happy to have him back on her side. "It is high time we fingered that landlord in The Pheasant. He gets some right dodgy characters in that pub of his and I'd like to have something to pin on him – know what I mean?"

"For the moment, all we are interested in is the drugs deal." Hilary cautioned severely. "Any problems with the landlord can wait. If he is allowing any nonsense on his premises, he will doubtless come again, so for the moment, let's stick to what we have. I don't know who is involved, but the gear is due to be handed over at nine this evening. Let's get it right and we should have an excellent result."

Maddox merely grinned wolfishly and led his companions away to change into civilian clothing.

Hilary glanced at her watch again. Ten to nine; by now the lads would be in place, doubtless enjoying an unexpected drink and keyed up with the prospect of imminent action. She just hoped that nothing would go wrong.

With another glance at her unresponsive timepiece, Sergeant Bedwell left her desk in search of a cup of coffee. As she went out of the office, she reflected a little sourly that frustrated waiting was very much part of a sergeant's job and would only get worse as she climbed the promotional ladder.

***

The Speckled Pheasant was a typical town pub, situated between narrow alleyways and containing the usual paraphernalia of juke box, fruit machines and cigarette vending machine. Despite the smoking ban, the walls were yellowed with ancient nicotine. Ancient hunting prints adorned the wall behind the juke box. Like most such establishments, it did a reasonable weekday trade, although it was never too busy and the usual clientele consisted of building workers and those few folk who lived right in the town itself. At nine in the evening, it was beginning to fill up and the smell of beer and unwashed bodies drifted between the two bars.

Jeff Maddox had little difficulty in deciding that Hilary's information had come from the man known as McConnel. Jeff had been in on the Whitehead raid and in spite of his antipathy toward the bearded hippy, he had been forced to concede that the intelligence had been excellent. Now it seemed that the blonde sergeant had produced the goods again and Maddox wondered what there could possibly be between Hilary and her unlikely informant. Surely she couldn't fancy the man. He was a scrote, just like all the other scrotes and if Abie Whitehead went down the road for a spell, it might be worthwhile letting him know who had provided the gen that sent him there.

Smiling at the thought, Maddox peeped through a window of the pub and the first person he saw was McConnel. The hippy sat sprawled on a bench in one corner and the big policeman was stunned. If he had provided the information, what was he doing on the scene? To make matters infinitely worse, if Maddox went inside, McConnel would recognise him instantly and that would ruin the entire operation. The big policeman wondered what to do. He had split up from his companions half an hour earlier and they would probably be in position already.

Tucking his chin into his collar, Maddox moved around the building and cautiously entered the almost empty lounge bar. An acne-spotted youth was moodily wiping glasses behind the counter and one other drinker looked up absently at his entrance. Quietly ordering a pint of local bitter, Maddox wondered how to get a message through to the others. Personal radios were useless in such a situation.

Taking his beer further up the bar counter, Maddox propped himself in one corner where an open serving hatch allowed him to see right through to the public bar. It wasn't an ideal position but it would do, providing him as it did a view of half the clientele and McConnel at his corner table. Maddox studied the sprawled drop out carefully, still unsure as to the reason for his presence.

The man known as McConnel was slumped across the table and looked very much the worse for wear. As always, the bobble hat was smeared across his lank hair and his desperately scruffy ensemble was enlivened by an emerald green neckerchief, peeking jauntily from the grimy collar of his shirt. He had a half filled glass in front of him but didn't look as though he was enjoying the drink. Even from where he stood, Maddox was aware of the man's slack posture and blank face. He was obviously stoned out of his mind and the policeman felt a fierce sense of anticipation.

Whether McConnel was involved in the drugs deal or not, Maddox was determined to make up for the humiliation of being ticked off in front of this bearded scumbag. No sergeant had any right to speak to him like that.

His sense of indignant righteousness almost made Jeff Maddox miss the entry of two more hippies, one of whom he instantly recognised.

"Spike Moroney by God!" The policeman breathed to himself. "If there are drugs involved anywhere in this town, that little fucker is bound to be in on it."

Moving around to get a better look at the newcomers, Maddox spotted his colleagues talking quietly in one corner and close to them was a small, well-dressed man who looked very familiar. Maddox couldn't immediately put a name to the face, but knew he had seen him before and watched as the man made a careful appraisal of all the people around him. He was an obvious villain, but villainy was hardly new in The Speckled Pheasant and there was nothing to link him with the impending drugs deal except for that sixth sense, enjoyed by only the most experienced policemen.

Dipping his face deep into his pint, Jeff Maddox watched the drama develop in the other room.

It was Moroney who made the first move. The dapper little man had studiously avoided him, but Spike pushed his way through a few people and tapped him on the shoulder.

"Hiya Razor." He greeted cheerfully and his voice was clearly audible even from the lounge bar. Maddox grinned happily. He knew who the little man was – of course he did. He should have recognised him immediately. Razor Wallace was well known to coppers throughout the county. Maddox heard him grunt a sour acknowledgement.

"'Ave you got the doins?" Spike went on in a loud whisper and the look he received from Wallace would have felled a cart horse. Looking suitably chastened, the hippy moved in closer to the little man and bent to whisper in his ear. Ignoring him, Wallace muttered an order to the waiting barman. With a full pint glass in his hand, he seemed to relax and after another good look around the smoky bar, he gestured to Spike and they moved across to a corner table on the opposite side of the room to McConnel. Spike's companion moved hesitantly after them and the two young bobbies watched with interest, their faces obscured by sleevers of beer.

McConnel didn't move from his corner and none of the other drinkers seemed at all interested in the oddly assorted trio of villains. Shady deals were normal practice in The Speckled Pheasant and the clientele knew better than to display any curiosity about the activities of others.

Scowling through the serving hatch, Maddox struggled to see what was going on. All he could see of the prospective drug deal was Razor Wallace's elegantly shod feet and Spike Moroney's beer glass moving animatedly as he spoke. With a muttered oath, the big fellow abandoned his observation post and moved into the public bar. He would have to risk being spotted by McConnel, although from the bearded hippy's posture, it didn't look as though he was in a fit state to see anything.

As he entered the public bar, a dart thudded into a board beside his head and Maddox flinched instinctively. In his absorption with the task in hand, he hadn't been looking where he was going and might well have found himself impaled against the wall.

"Watch where you're bloody well going, Mate." Growled the dart thrower, a burly farm labourer; "I nearly had you there."

Maddox hastily apologised, cursing inwardly at drawing attention to himself. His colleagues looked up at his entrance but Wallace and the two hippies appeared absorbed in their haggling, while the crusty in the corner seemed to be fast asleep.

In fact McConnel was wide awake and suddenly very worried. He had immediately spotted the two young coppers for what they were and seen Maddox hurry into the lounge bar. He couldn't help an inward smirk at the near accident with the dart, but sobered quickly. He had expected the cops, but Spike's trading partner was another matter. Razor Wallace was a big city criminal and a very dangerous man. McConnel had come across him in the past and knew that wherever Wallace went, he left a trail of bloody unhappiness in his wake. A petty but extremely violent villain, he had a string of previous convictions ranging from shoplifting to a bungled but very unpleasant armed robbery. Two people had been badly injured in the robbery and one of them was a seventy year old woman who would never walk again. Wallace had been sentenced to seven years for that particular crime, but in one of the ironies of the penal system had been out in three to resume his life of petty villainy.

He had earned the nickname 'Razor' in the early nineties when he used a blade embedded in a magazine on an unfortunate derelict, foolish enough to boast about the hidden riches he professed to possess. That the man hadn't a penny to his name hadn't saved him from months of painful hospital treatment that gave him time to reflect on the folly of putting on airs with the likes of Razor Wallace.

McConnel watched the low-voiced conversation across the room and wondered whether to take a hand in proceedings. He might have done so had PC Maddox not been watching him so intently. The big policeman's presence kept McConnel away from the action.

McConnel's feeling about passing information to Hilary Bedwell had suddenly become horribly ambivalent. It wasn't his job or his intention to assist the police and he had only done it for the girl herself. Now it looked like going very wrong. Ellie was right, he thought. He was making a fool of himself.

There was nothing he could do about it at that stage though and he continued watching carefully from behind half closed eyelids. The young cops looked a tough pair and Maddox could obviously look after himself. So could Wallace, but neither Spike nor Robbie stood any chance in a brawl and McConnel knew he was going to have to get involved whether he liked it or not. Before he could move however, the action started and it was too late.

Once again looking carefully around the room, Razor Wallace withdrew a small packet from the inside pocket of his suit. This he handed to Spike who immediately produced a roll of grubby banknotes. The grimy youth was so pleased at concluding the sale that he didn't bother to check that he was unobserved.

From the moment of handover, everything moved with almost frightening speed. The young coppers quickly crossed the room with Maddox hard on their heels. Sensing trouble, the barman moved toward his telephone, then paused as Maddox flashed a warrant card in passing. The other customers watched in open-mouthed astonishment as the forces of law and order closed in on their quarry.

Robbie who had been an absorbed witness to the dealing between Spike and Wallace was the first to sense danger. Looking up, he caught Jeff Maddox' eye and began to rise from his seat, only to be smashed down by a heavy hand. Before Razor Wallace could react, one of the younger officers had handcuffs on his wrists and had lifted two exhibits expertly from a jacket pocket. Spike was similarly tethered while Robbie sat in numbed horror, not at all sure what he had got himself into. It was possibly as well that he was even more stoned than his mentor, watching helplessly from the far corner.

Seeing that there was not going to be any violence and that he couldn't do anything about it anyway, McConnel slipped from his seat but he wasn't quite quick enough. Having seen that his colleagues were in control of the situation, Maddox was on his way back. McConnel had taken only two paces when a brawny hand slammed into his elbow, twisting the arm up painfully behind his back.

"Stay where you are, Toe Rag." The big policeman gritted. "The only place you are going is down to the nick with the rest of them – know what I mean?"

McConnel made himself relax. He knew that Maddox wouldn't hesitate to break his arm. Turning slowly around, he smiled blearily at the policeman.

"I was merely going home Officer." He jerked his chin at the empty glass. "As you see, I have finished my drink and as this place seems to attract all the wrong sort of clientele nowadays…."

"Save it for the Beak, Arsehole." Maddox growled. "Perhaps he still believes in Father Christmas."

Manhandling his captive across the room, Maddox took charge of the situation.

"Hang on to the sergeant's fancy man here." He snapped at one of the youngsters. "I'll deal with the rest of them.

'Just don't let the bastard go or you will be deep in the shit."

He gave McConnel a shove that jerked his shoulder up into its socket and brought an exclamation of pain from the bearded mouth. The constable looked curiously at him, not really understanding what Maddox was getting at.

Once Spike, Robbie and the angrily protesting drug dealer had been taken through to the publican's quarters, transport had been called for and the exhibits duly recorded in his notebook by PC Maddox himself, the big man turned his attention back to McConnel.

"Right you." He spoke with grim relish. "I want a personal word."

McConnel shrugged, his expression bland.

"Any time you like, PC Maddox. I don't know what I am supposed to have done but I'm certainly not involved with these three."

"That's right." Spike began loyally, but his words were cut off by a painful dig in the ribs from the man who held him captive. Maddox was unimpressed.

"Cut out the humour." He snapped and bundled the unprotesting hippy out of the building and into the cold night air. As he went through the door, he was pulling his truncheon out of his pocket and his colleagues looked blankly at each other. One of them shrugged and they turned back to their shaken but still volubly protesting prisoners.

Ten minutes later the sound of a siren announced the arrival of transport and Jeff Maddox reappeared. His truncheon was back in his pocket and he looked pleased with himself.

"The scumbag was right, Fellas." he announced to his colleagues. "He wasn't involved after all, so I've sent him home and we can interview him in due course – know what I mean?"

"Was that wise Jeff?" PC Derek Whittingham frowned and Maddox turned irritably on him.

"It was what to do Son. I know where he lives and he won't move from there for a while. Come on, let's get these arseholes tucked up for the night, then we'll have a beer to celebrate."

CHAPTER FOUR

Hilary Bedwell felt the familiar rush of triumphant elation, attendant on all successful operations. Watching through a one-way mirror, she couldn't help grinning as Wallace and the two hippies were booked into the 'custody suite' and the small cache of drugs was listed by the custody sergeant.

"Three dozen white tablets – probably ecstasy or speed." He said expressionlessly, holding the transparent sachet up to the light as he did so. "One envelope containing six smaller packets of white powder." He raised his eyebrows at Wallace but the drug dealer declined to answer the unspoken question.

"Never mind; they can go along to the lab with the rest of the gear."

He continued writing in laborious longhand into his ledger.

"Three cachets of blue, pink and yellow tablets – where did you get the poppers from, Razor?"

Wallace shrugged and the sergeant grinned up at Jeff Maddox and his companions who flanked the sorry collection of villains.

"Last of all, six paper twists of cannabis leaf. Bit of a come down for you, hey Razor? I thought you were only in to the hard stuff. Didn't you once tell me that 'shit is only for the shit eaters?'"

"Piss off."

Wallace looked murderous but the sergeant was unabashed.

"Never mind, I suppose our worthy chancellor's fiscal policies are affecting us all – even those who deal in this sort of crap."

Half an hour later, the three miscreants were safely locked away and Hilary was back in her office holding a cheerful debrief with her colleagues.

"That was a good evenings work, Chaps," she told them brightly. "We've got those three worthies well and truly sewn up and I shall have to see about a small reward from CID for my informant."

"And a beer or three for the lads, Sarge?" Maddox asked the question and Hilary smiled at him.

"Of course Jeff. I'll set them up as soon as we go off duty. I want your statements before you go though."

"Ah come on Sarge; those can surely wait till tomorrow?"

Hilary glanced at her watch.

"We've still got an hour or so till we knock off and they aren't going to be complicated are they? Surely you can get them done in that time?"

Maddox looked sullen but she was determined to have her way. Before the big man could comment further, the telephone on her desk rang and Hilary picked up the receiver.

After announcing herself, she listened quietly and a small frown appeared between her eyes.

"Where?" She asked. "How badly hurt?"

The conversation over, she replaced the receiver and turned slowly back to Maddox, the frown still in place.

"That was the Control Room," she told her suddenly attentive audience. "They have received a report of a traveller beaten up in the alley that runs beside The Speckled Pheasant. The ambulance has been called but apparently the bloke is in a bad way.

'You didn't see anything while you were there I suppose?"

"That must have been…" Mark Webber began eagerly, then stopped as Maddox looked angrily across at him.

"Must have been what, PC Webber?" Hilary broke the ensuing silence and her tone was grim. A horrible suspicion was forming in her mind, although she couldn't quite believe what she was thinking.

"Must have been what those scrotes were waiting for." Maddox put in but Hilary's attention was focussed on the younger officer.

"Must have been what, PC Webber?" She repeated bleakly and the young man looked uncomfortable.

"I dunno Sarge. I just thought it…" he broke off, not knowing what to say. Hilary turned back to Maddox.

"Is there something you blokes aren't telling me, Jeff? Who else was in The Pheasant this evening?"

The big man shrugged.

"Nobody really. Oh there were the usual yobbos about. You know what that place is like. A couple of scumbags probably had a fall out – it often happens. You know that Skipper."

Hilary looked doubtful and her face set in grim lines.

"I think there is more to this than you are telling me," she said slowly. "You lot are covering something up and I'm going to find out what it is.

'I'm going down to The Pheasant now and PC Webber, you can come with me."

"But what about our reports Sarge?" Maddox grinned and she turned on him angrily.

"You weren't so keen to do your bloody reports a moment or two ago, PC Maddox and besides, you don't need PC Webber to do yours for you.

'I want to know what is going on and if you won't tell me I shall have to find out for myself. You two can hang on here until we get back."

"Don't be too long Sarge or the beer will get warm." Maddox said facetiously but she was unimpressed.

"That will be just too bad," she snapped. "Just make sure you are still here when we get back."

It was only a short walk to The Speckled Pheasant and it was accomplished in a grimly uncomfortable silence. A flashing blue light guided them around one side of the pub and as they arrived, two paramedics were manhandling a stretcher into the back of the waiting ambulance while a third held a drip above the unconscious casualty. A small group of onlookers stood silently watching the drama and Hilary pushed her way through them and approached the ambulance men.

"What's the story Chaps?" She asked and the senior medic turned to her.

"Hello Sergeant," his eyes took in the stripes on her arm. "A bad 'un I'm afraid. This geezer has been done over good and proper and while he doesn't look much of a bloke, someone went a bit over the top, I reckon."

"Mind if I take a look?"

Not waiting for a reply, she stepped forward and shone her torch down on the patient. He had an oxygen mask over his face, but even in the torch light, there was no mistaking the lank hair and tangled beard of the man she knew as McConnel. The woollen bobble hat was still in place, but it was sodden with blood and his face was swollen and gashed above both eyes. His nose looked as though it was broken and blood had congealed at the sides of his mouth. Hilary felt herself engulfed by an enormous wave of compassion as she looked down on the unconscious man.

"Do you know who he is then, Sarge?"

The ambulance man spoke quietly and she nodded, too angry to speak. Turning away, she glanced at Mark Webber and the young constable's stricken expression told her all she needed to know.

"Yes, I know him well," she said shortly. "I'll arrange for his relatives to be informed and PC Webber can accompany him to the hospital. We will need a statement as soon as he comes round."

"Doesn't seem worth the hassle for his sort." Another medic put in and she turned on him angrily.

"He is a human being just like you and me, so we treat 'his sort,'" the words were angrily snapped, "just the same as anyone else and don't you forget it."

The man looked at her in open astonishment.

"Sorry Sergeant," he muttered and concentrated on the job in hand. Moments later, McConnel was installed in the ambulance with PC Webber sitting uncomfortably beside him. The doors closed, the three paramedics climbed into the front of the vehicle and it howled away into the night.

Hilary Bedwell was grimly thoughtful as she returned alone to the police station.

CHAPTER FIVE

Dank white fog hung over the clearing as Hilary parked the police car as close as she could get to the red bus. The forest was silent and in spite of her normal pragmatism, Hilary felt a shiver run through her body and it wasn't due entirely to the cold.

It was a few minutes short of midnight and the Beacon encampment was eerily silent. In the distance, a dog barked fretfully and Hilary took a deep breath before moving purposefully toward the bus. Climbing the three rickety steps that hung below the doorway, she rapped hard with her knuckles.

"Hello, is anyone at home?" She called and her voice seemed to echo emptily through the fog.

Inside the bus, a dog barked sharply and she remembered the shaggy brute that had taken a bite at Jeff Maddox. In spite of her preoccupation, Hilary smiled grimly at the memory.

"Open up please," she called again. "It's the police."

After what seemed an interminable time, she heard movement within the vehicle and allowed herself to relax slightly as she thought about what to say.

A candle glowed fitfully within the bus and after another long period of silence during which Hilary felt her temper rising, the door opened slowly in front of her. Framed in the aperture was the sullen-faced female she had seen on her initial visit to The Beacon. The girl was dressed in a grimy nightgown that reached down to her knees and her face was puffy with interrupted sleep. The expression in her eyes was anything but welcoming.

"Wot do you want then?" She demanded and Hilary moved up a step so that she would not have to look upward when she spoke.

"May I come in?" She asked quietly and fear flared momentarily in the girl's eyes.

"Wot for? Wot's 'appened now?"

"Nothing serious." Hilary soothed. "There has been a bit of trouble but it isn't too bad. Let me in and I will tell you all about it."

Stepping reluctantly aside with a scowl on her face, the girl allowed the police sergeant to enter the bus. As she did so, the dank, musty odour of the interior hit Hilary like a blow to the face. It was foetid and claustrophobic but she tried hard to prevent her disgust from showing. It wouldn't do to antagonise the girl even more at this stage. Momentarily she wondered how a man like McConnell could live in such an atmosphere, then she banished the thought. This was not the time to be anything other than thoroughly professional.

The dog looked briefly up at her from where it lay across the doorway, effectively blocking the entrance. The heavy tail wagged briefly, then the animal dropped its head on to its paws and went back to sleep. A baby muttered from deep within the interior of the bus, but it was hidden in the shadows and Hilary couldn't see it. With an effort, she stepped over the supine animal and turned to face McConnel's woman, who stood in a somewhat confrontational pose in front of the doorway.

"Okay, yore in as you wanted. Now tell me wot's 'appened to McConnel. It's 'im yore 'ere about, innit? Wot's 'e dun now?"

Hilary nodded briefly.

"I am sorry My Dear, but there has been an accident and he is in hospital I'm afraid. I don't think he is badly hurt, but he will probably be in for a day or two."

"Wot 'appened?"

Looking a little desperately for somewhere to sit, Hilary shook her head.

"We don't know. It looks as though he has been beaten up, but as yet we haven't discovered who did it."

"Nor will you neither," the girl spat bitterly. "You don't care about people like McConnel. If it 'ad been anyone else, you'd 'ave found out by now, but becos you look on us as a load of scum, you won't do a bloody thing an' you can't tell me any different, Sergeant sodding Bedwell."

She glared at Hilary and the candlelight highlighted the glimmer of tears in her eyes. In spite of her disgust at the squalid condition of the bus, Hilary felt intense compassion for the girl. She was one of the lost people, the ones who are forgotten by society and to a certain extent, she was correct in the way she thought. In normal circumstances, the assault on McConnel would be written off as a domestic incident and quickly forgotten.

But these were not normal circumstances. She knew in her heart that McConnel had been beaten up for helping her and she therefore had a personal stake in the matter. It would not be brushed under the carpet, of that she was grimly determined. Sighing in frustration, she turned her attention back to the girl.

"I don't want to squabble with you Girl and I can understand your feelings, but I promise you that this incident will be investigated as carefully as any other assault that occurs. I will personally ensure that whoever beat McConnel up will be prosecuted with the full force of the law."

Even to her own ears, the words sounded pompous and affected, while the girl was totally unimpressed.

"'At's only cos you fancy 'im yoreself innit?"

The all too close to the mark question threw Hilary completely and she changed tack as fast as she could.

"What is your name, Love?"

"Why d'you wanna know?"

She sighed with exasperation.

"Because I am trying to help you damn it! I came here to inform you of McConnel's accident, not to argue with you. I am quite happy to take you in to the hospital if you would like to see him. I am on your side you know, so try not to fight with me please."

Interest flared momentarily in the pudgy little face, but it was quickly overshadowed by the innate suspicion of one who has no reason to trust the police.

"Why should you wanna do that then? Wot's in it fer you?"

She looked crafty for a moment.

"It is becos you fancy 'im yoreself innit? You've got yore eyes on my man and it's probly cos of you that 'e got 'urt anyway."

The words were close enough to the truth to make Hilary feel very uncomfortable, but she made no attempt to hide her exasperation.

Of course I don't fancy him, you silly creature. The only interest I have in McConnel is that of a police officer with a particularly troublesome member of the community. For all that, he has rights too and I will ensure that they are seen to. In the meantime I am offering to help you out of the goodness of my heart, not for any other reason.

"Now, are you bloody coming with me or shall I leave you here?"

"Wot'll I do with the kids?"

"I don't know, Girl. That is your problem. I am offering you a lift to the hospital and a chance to see your man. I am not going to arrange a bloody babysitter for you as well. I have enough on my plate as it is.

'Now let me ask again – what is your name?"

"Ellie."

It was said with less petulance than before and Hilary wondered whether she was getting through to the girl at last. Ellie was probably more accustomed to being cursed at than to kindness of any sort. Hilary kept her face blank when she spoke again.

"Okay Ellie: why don't you wake up one of your neighbours. There must be someone around here who will keep an eye on the children for you surely? Anyway, I'll give you five minutes to arrange something and get some clothes on, then I am on my way."

Without another word, the girl adjusted the front of her nightgown then pushed past Hilary into the darkness. A moment later, the sergeant heard her calling out to someone else.

'Just like a bloody council estate,' she thought sourly to herself. 'Everyone knows everyone else's business, but there is always someone on hand to help if the need arises.'

A few minutes later, Ellie was back, an eager look on her face and her original apathy replaced with an air of brisk efficiency.

"Spike an' Robbie aren't 'ome yet, so Julie and Red'll look after the brats," she told Hilary as she changed into the same worn clothing that she had been wearing when Hilary had seen her last. "I told 'em we might be a while an' they don't seem to mind like."

"Good, let's go then."

With mild surprise, Hilary noticed the girl glance at her reflection in a mottled mirror and carefully adjust her tangled hair into some semblance of order with her fingers. Then she was ready and two minutes later, they drove off into the night on their way to see McConnel in hospital.

Behind them the Beacon Community slept on in the drifting fog.

***

"That bloody half-arsed woman has gone too bloody far this time – know what I mean?"

The speaker was Jeff Maddox and he was angrily sounding off to Mark Webber and Derek Whittingham, the two young bobbies who had been with him on the drugs raid. The object of his invective was Sergeant Hilary Bedwell and the younger men listened in wide-eyed amazement.

It was well after the scheduled end of their shift, their reports on the incident had been done and were waiting on Sergeant Bedwell's desk, but the sergeant herself had not returned from her visit to the hospital. They wanted to go home but she had told them to wait and even Maddox was wary about directly disobeying her orders.

The three men were in the bar of the Police Club, perched high on top of the station building. All three nursed pints of beer and apart from the barman, they were alone. The time had progressed well beyond the normal hour for closing. Peering gloomily into the depths of his glass, Maddox wondered how to get his own back on the blonde sergeant.

"Who the hell does she think she is?" He demanded of nobody in particular. "A snotty little wench only just out of training school and she tries to tell me how police work should be done. That just isn't right – know what I mean?"

"You were a bit rough on that scrote, Jeff." Webber put in hesitantly. "I thought you had sent him home, so I was pretty damned gobsmacked to see him being shoved into the back of the blood wagon. He looked a total write off too, I can tell you."

"Served the fucker right," Maddox growled. "He has been asking for a good hiding for ages – know what I mean?"

Before driving out to The Beacon, Hilary had arranged for Webber to be relieved at the hospital and given him strict instructions to wait at the station till she returned. The young man had wasted no time in getting back to his companions and telling them exactly how McConnel looked.

"I reckon he'll be in there for weeks," he finished off and Maddox scowled furiously.

"Serves the filthy little arsehole right." He muttered. "He gave me trouble so I just whacked him a few times – know what I mean? Anyone would have done the same in the circumstances and at least we know the scumbag won't hassle us again.

'Anyway, nobody can prove it if we all keep our traps shut. It's his word against mine – know what I mean?"

They knew what he meant but both young men looked uncomfortable at the knowledge. Although both were probationers and a little in awe of an experienced copper like Maddox, they were far more afraid of Sergeant Bedwell whose wrath, once aroused was reputed to be frightening.

"So you lads just keep shtum and it'll all blow over in a couple of days." Maddox cautioned severely. "Now let's go home for Christ's sake. We've done our work for the night and God only knows what has happened to that snotty little bitch. Probably getting all lovey dovey with her poor bloody crusty – know what I mean? She is welcome to the bastard too, but she can't expect us to wait here all fucking night, just so she can have it off with the scumbag."

"But what is Sergeant Bedwell going to say if we go, Jeff? She told us we had to wait."

"Sergeant ruddy Bedwell can bloody well lump it Fellas. You can stay on if you like but I'm not hanging around here all night so that she can get her fucking rocks off. Besides, you can bet a pound to a pinch of the proverbial that she won't authorise overtime, even if we stay till sodding breakfast"

Without another word, Jeff Maddox lumbered from the club, a heavy, dangerous man whose anger made him twice as dangerous. The younger men followed somewhat hesitantly in his wake..

With a sigh of resignation, the Club Steward whipped their empty glasses from the counter and piled them into a sink full of soapy water. He had been listening in to the conversation and wondered what Jeff Maddox had been up to this time.

***

"I suppose you can see him for a moment, Sergeant, but don't stay too long. He isn't supposed to have visitors yet."

Hilary smiled her thanks to the night nurse, who somewhat reluctantly led her and Ellie to a screened off bed in one corner of the ward.

McConnel was conscious, but he looked a sorry sight. A drip cradle above his bed pumped life saving fluids into his system and he had tubes running into both nostrils. One heavily bandaged arm lay across his chest and he looked up at his visitors from a mass of livid welts and bruises. Hilary tried to keep the shock from her eyes, but Ellie burst into anguished tears.

"Oh McConnel, wot 'ave they done to you?" She wailed and Hilary put a finger to her lips to silence her.

"Hush Ellie; we'll be thrown out of here if you make too much noise." She warned but the girl threw herself across the man in the bed, making him grimace with the sudden pain. When he glanced across at Hilary, the mocking glint was back in his eye.

"You people play pretty rough, Sergeant Bedwell," he murmured and she was forced to bend over so that her ear was close to his mouth before she could hear what he was saying.

"Who did it McConnel?" She asked grimly once she understood but he shook his head slowly.

"My problem and I will sort it out my own way," he said. "Thanks for getting hold of Ellie."

The eyes still glinted and Hilary wasn't sure whether he meant what he was saying or merely being sarcastic, but she let it be. Feeling somehow traitorous to her own kind, she stayed beside the bed for a full five minutes, looking down at McConnel and the weeping girl while her mind explored the ridiculous nature of the situation.

Here was she – a grown woman holding down a responsible job with a great future ahead of her and putting it all in jeopardy by making a fool of herself over a dirty, drug-ruined drop out. He was now part of an official enquiry, which made matters a little easier, but in her heart, Hilary knew that her interest went considerably deeper than that.

She could not explain it though, not even to herself. Hilary had never had any real interest in men, knowing that she wanted to be a career copper rather than a housewife. There had been the odd moment of passion in her teens and at training school, she had fallen under the spell of a muscular instructor, but that had all been purely physical. She had always wanted to be a police officer and now she was married to her job. She had done well and was determined to go right to the top, so what on earth was she doing, jeopardising her chances by acting stupidly with an awful specimen like McConnel? It wasn't merely foolish, it was criminal! She had to pull herself together.

Suiting action to the thought, she put a firm hand on Ellie's shoulder.

"Come on Ellie Love. We had better leave him to it. We all need sleep and you can visit again tomorrow."

Ellie submitted weakly and moved toward the door. As Hilary turned to follow, McConnel reached out with his good arm and grabbed hold of her hand. His palm felt hard and calloused against her skin, but she felt that familiar tingling in her blood at his touch.

"Thank you Sergeant Bedwell," he breathed and once again she was forced to move close in order to hear. With their faces mere inches apart, the smell of his body was rank, but for some reason it excited rather than repelled her. "Thanks for telling Ellie and bringing her along. You didn't have to do that."

"It is part of my job McConnel," she told him severely. "I did it for her, not you."

"Will you be coming again yourself?"

She shook her head.

"Probably not McConnel, although I will make sure that Ellie has transport to bring her in to see you tomorrow.

'Mind you," she smiled at the sudden spurt of disappointment in his eyes, "we will be needing a full statement from you as soon as you are fit enough and I might have to take it myself."

Smiling tightly, he lay back on the pillow, tension visibly draining from his body.

"You are one hell of a nice lady, Sergeant Bedwell." He murmured before his eyes closed and he was asleep.

"Nice – just 'nice'? What sort of a compliment is that?" She whispered to herself, but with her spirits lifted and her confusion considerably increased, Sergeant Hilary Bedwell hurried out of the hospital in search of Ellie.

CHAPTER SIX

Hilary frowned at the paper in her hand and an angry flush rose to her cheeks. She had come on duty half an hour early in order to catch up on her paperwork and the first thing she had found in her mail basket was the report that was now causing her considerable indignation.

She had written the report herself and it was a request to be considered for specialist musketry training. In spite of her genteel background, Hilary had been brought up with firearms and knew herself to be an excellent shot. Her father, the Bishop was a keen sportsman and Hilary had handled shotguns and sporting rifles throughout her formative years. Proving her adaptability to all aspects of policing could only enhance her promotion prospects, so she was determined to make a name for herself as part of the county's armed response team, somewhat derisively known as 'The Cowboys' or 'Flak jackets' by other policemen.

It had been a lucidly expressed report and in it, she had pointed out her considerable qualifications for the job to which she was aspiring. She had proved her tactical competence on the special course at Bramshill Police College and with her record, there could be no doubting her mental toughness. At the time of submission, she had been confident that her request would be granted.

In fact it had not. The Assistant Chief Constable had penned his views at the foot of the report and it was these somewhat caustic comments that brought the flush to Hilary's cheeks.

'Why is it,' the ACC had written, 'that those officers coming to us from eminent seats of learning always seem to feel a need to walk around like Wyatt Earp or modern day Rambos? This sergeant has already shown that she has an excellent brain, so I cannot understand what she is trying to prove by volunteering for hazardous duties. Her application is therefore refused.'

Hilary scowled bitterly at the wall, her face pinched with anger and her sense of injustice threatening to provoke her into a tantrum. She knew that the ACC's comments were unfair and guessed that they were probably motivated by his well known misogynistic tendencies. He was very much a copper of the old school and as the only female graduate in the county, she had been exposed to his sarcasm on previous occasions. Sexism was very much part of police culture and when she had joined, Hilary had gradually grown accustomed to being asked 'and do you?' whenever she was introduced by name. On the first occasion, she had made the mistake of querying the comment with a grizzled sergeant and he had chortled with glee.

"Bed well, Lass. Are you a good fuck?"

She remembered blushing furiously, but having the presence of mind to respond in kind.

"You will never know will you, Sergeant?" The man had left her alone after that, but the feeling that as a woman, she was regarded as a second class citizen had persisted through her years of service. And now this nonsense from no less a personage than the Assistant Chief Constable? Hilary was more than a little upset.

"Modern day Rambo indeed! I'll show the sexist idiot about Wyatt Earp."

Determined not to allow her application to be bludgeoned into obscurity by a mere man, Hilary jumped to her feet. She would make her feelings known to the Guv'nor and if he wouldn't do anything about it, she would go over his head to the Divisional Superintendent. If he couldn't or wouldn't help, she would go higher – perhaps even to the Chief Constable himself.

Her bitter musings were interrupted by a uniformed constable who stuck his head through the door.

"Guv'nor wants to see you right away Sarge." The young man said. "Seems to have his knickers in a knot about something."

"Good; I want to see him too. Hilary muttered and with the abortive application in her hand, she hurried down the corridor to knock on the door marked 'Station Chief Inspector.'

***

"What the hell is going on, Sergeant Bedwell?"

The Station Chief Inspector was not in a good mood. Hilary had burst into his office, determined to have her say, but she wasn't given a chance. The Great Man was in an obvious temper and without even bothering to ask her to sit, tore into the attack. Somewhat nonplussed she stood in front of him, not quite knowing what to say.

"What…. What do you mean, Sir?"

He didn't seem to notice her sudden attack of nervousness. His big face was flushed with anger and she could see a vein pulsing in his neck above the starched white collar.

"I mean, Sergeant Bedwell…." he paused for effect; "…I mean these stories that have come to my notice about my best and most promising sergeant having it off with a member of the New Age brigade – a bloody drop out of a crusty for Christ's sake!"

It was Hilary's turn to flush and her original complaint forgotten, she struggled to control the crimson tide that rose to her cheeks. This was totally ridiculous and in danger of getting out of hand. Her eyes flashing fire, she leaned over Chief Inspector Bolton's desk until her face was only a few inches from his own.

"I have not heard any such stories, Sir and if I do, I can assure you that I will have the story teller's guts for knitting wool before the day is out. Perhaps you ought to pay me the courtesy of telling me just what has been said about me before flying off the handle?"

Chief Inspector Bolton narrowed his eyes and gestured somewhat wearily to a chair in front of the desk. Hilary sat down gratefully for her knees were trembling with emotion. Her notoriously irascible superior went on in a calmer voice.

"Don't blame me for getting angry, Sergeant Bedwell. Like everyone else in this nick, I have high hopes for you and expect you to go a long way in the police service. However, when I hear that my most promising officer is playing the fool with a scumbag from the travelling fraternity, I can't help getting a little bit hot under the collar.

'Now tell me exactly what has been going on to start off all these rumours – scurrilous though they might be."

"They aren't true, Sir," she said quietly. "They are not true and I would like to know who has been putting them about. Besides, he isn't even a traveller – not a proper one at any rate."

Sighing audibly, Bolton leaned back in his chair and looked levelly across the desk at his discomfited sergeant.

"You worry me, Sergeant Bedwell, you really do. Even if I accept that you know nothing about these rumours, you obviously know exactly what they are about. Does that mean there is some basic element of truth in them after all?"

Without waiting for her to reply he went on somewhat ominously.

"Let me tell you, young woman, that rumour and gossip have been responsible for ruining more than a few promising police careers. I do not want to see the same thing happen with you.

'You are an outstanding officer, Hilary Bedwell, but if there is any substance at all to the stories that are doing the rounds, I would suggest you do something about it and pretty damned quickly. I do not want to interfere in your personal life, but bear in mind that you cannot afford to be the subject of gossip at this stage in your career.

'Great things are predicted for you Sergeant, but there are always officers who will be only too pleased to see you come to grief. We are an old fashioned service and most coppers feel that there is no substitute for experience in the job. You and the other whiz kids who take short cuts to the top of the tree are viewed with considerable suspicion, no matter how good you might be at the job. You have an additional disadvantage in that you are a good-looking female. I know it isn't fair, but that in itself makes you vulnerable and well…"

He spread his big hands apart in a gesture of helplessness and Hilary knew only too well that he was right. Jeff Maddox and company were not the major problem. They were minor cogs in the great machine of the police service and the ones she really had to watch were the faceless senior officers, many of whom would be only too pleased to see her fall from grace.

"I can assure you Sir that I am not 'having it off' with the man in question. My relationship with him is purely that of copper and snout."

"The Abie Whitehead job?" Bolton raised bushy eyebrows and Hilary nodded.

"Yes Sir, and the drugs bust that nailed Razor Wallace. He gave me the gen on both of those cases."

Bolton nodded, obviously mollified if not entirely satisfied.

"Okay Sergeant, he is obviously on the level with the information he supplies and you had better register him as an official snout, but for God's sake don't go giving anyone reason to talk. You know how coppers love a hint of scandal."

"I won't Sir," she promised fervently and he waved a hand in weary dismissal. As she reached the door, he called her back.

"Ah, Hilary, can your bloke tell us anything about the Thursday breaker perhaps?"

"Thursday Joe, Sir? I don't know. I never actually ask him for information. He just comes up and gives it to me. I can ask him about Thursday Joe if you like?"

For many months there had been a series of housebreakings in the residential areas of the town. Each one took place in broad daylight and every one was on a Thursday afternoon. Extra manpower had been called in, CID had made a major effort and the areas concerned had been flooded with plain clothes officers from other stations. Still the culprit had never been found. The nickname had been given to him when a young officer had referred to 'that Joe who does the drums on Thursdays' and so Thursday Joe he had become.

Chief Inspector Bolton shook his head.

"Just go on as normal with him Sergeant. He is obviously a snout worth cultivating and you don't want to scare him off by deviating from his normal procedure. What is the story on this scrote who was beaten up last night?"

This time it was Hilary who shook her head.

"I'm not sure, Sir. The man was badly hurt and taken to hospital but I don't know the full story yet. I informed his girlfriend and took her down there in the early hours, but he was too groggy for an interview. I'll get a statement from him at the hospital in an hour or so."

"Make sure it is a detailed one, Sergeant. Punch ups so close to the town centre give us all a bad name."

With that, the interview was over and the Chief Inspector gave her a last searching look.

"Did you have something for me when you came in Sergeant?" He glanced pointedly at the now crumpled sheet of paper in Hilary's hand, but she shook her head in weary resignation.

"It wasn't anything important, Sir. It really doesn't matter."

Hilary left the Chief Inspector's office with a deep sense of injustice and a burning desire to prove her detractors wrong.

"PC Maddox," she called as she passed through the control room, "I want you to drive me down to the hospital. There is someone we both need a word with."

Jeff Maddox, who had been studying a computer printout looked up with an expression of nervous surprise on his face. He knew who Hilary was referring to and so did everyone else in the room. Rumours about the pretty sergeant, the man known as McConnel and the events of the previous night had been flying around the station all day. There was silence in the room as the big constable followed Hilary to her office and it was broken by one of the younger radio operators. Sitting up very straight in his chair, he beamed at the people around him.

"Well I'll be buggered with a bent broomstick." He said to nobody in particular. "This really is getting interesting."

The other operators bent pointedly to their computer screens and the hum of normal activity returned to the control room.

***

"I am sorry," the ward sister told Hilary. "He discharged himself in the early hours of this morning."

"Was he alright?" Hilary frowned. "I mean.. I thought his injuries were quite serious. When I saw him around midnight, he looked as though he was in a hell of a state."

Glancing quickly at Jeff Maddox she was relieved to note that he didn't seem to have picked up on that particular bit of information.

"He was in a hell of a state Sergeant, but he took it upon himself to leave. Didn't tell a soul and slipped away without anyone seeing him. Even the chap in the next bed didn't notice him go. He says he didn't at any rate."

She frowned and Hilary couldn't help smiling at her aggrieved expression. She glanced across at Maddox but the big man's face was impassive.

"We'll find him Sister," she promised. "I'll try and persuade him to come back and get himself seen to properly."

Maddox drove out to The Beacon in an affronted silence and Hilary made no effort to lighten the atmosphere. She was still bitterly angry about the brutal treatment McConnel had received and was determined to ensure that the burly PC beside her was adequately punished. That he had been the one to administer the beating, she had no doubt. His manner and the reaction of the two younger officers to news of McConnel's injuries had been just too obvious. Her interview with the Chief Inspector and the stories that were obviously circulating behind her back made her all the more determined to have everything out in the open.

For once the sun was shining as they drove into the clearing and in its cheerful rays, the old red bus looked more decrepit than ever. Maddox parked the police car under a tree and the two officers moved together towards McConnel's home.

The big dog still slept on the end of its rope and the mucky-nosed toddler was again playing between the wheels, but Maddox did not repeat his previous mistake and ignored the mite. Soulful blue eyes watched them move past and the child dug diligently at its nose. Hilary looked hurriedly away.

Ellie opened the door to them almost immediately and grudgingly admitted that McConnel was at home. He lay on a mattress, set up in the middle of the floor and Hilary couldn't help a rush of concern at his appearance. In the cold light of day, he looked considerably worse than he had the night before.

Bare-chested, he still wore the silly little bobble hat and she briefly wondered whether he ever took it off. He watched them approach his bed through badly blackened eyes, the hard ridges of stitched flesh very apparent around his forehead. His nose was bent to one side and there was a livid bruise down the length of his jawbone. In spite of his battered appearance, the green eyes twinkled at the police officers.

"Well, well – visitors so soon," he murmured through grossly thickened lips. "The lovely Sergeant Bedwell and her tame gorilla no less. We mustn't keep meeting like this Sergeant or people will talk, but what can I do for you this time?"

Maddox tensed visibly at the mocking humour but Hilary kept her face rigidly impassive.

"You can go back to hospital for a start, McConnel. We have just come from there and everyone is upset that you discharged yourself. You need treatment, Man. I understand that you have a broken rib and a badly strained wrist as well as the visible bruising. With your face in that state, you probably have a touch of concussion as well. You might not feel too bad, but you are not well, McConnel and you need a few days to recover."

"What a lovely medical missionary you would have made, Sergeant." Although it was difficult to hear what he was saying, there could be no doubt about the mockery in his tone. "Still," he shrugged and winced at the pain of the gesture, "medicine's loss can only be of inestimable benefit to the police service.

'Your concern for my welfare is appreciated, but why on earth did you bring Tonto with you? I had been looking forward to a chat and I don't suppose he knows much about civilised conversation."

He smiled crookedly as he spoke, but his eyes were cold and almost white as he glanced at Maddox. The policeman tensed again and seemed about to explode, but Hilary touched his elbow and he made a visible effort to relax. The injured man was unrepentant.

"Mind you, they do say that criminals will always revisit the scene of their crime, don't they? Do you think that might extend to visiting their victims as well?"

Ellie watched anxiously from the doorway, her face very pale and her eyes screwed up as she tried to follow the conversation. Noticing a gauzy pink curtain that seemed to partition off one corner of the bus, Hilary gestured to it in an effort to cool the atmosphere.

"What's that, Ellie?" She turned to the girl. "Children's bedroom?"

McConnel laughed harshly and there was no humour in the sound.

"We sleep together in our society, Sergeant. Why should the kids have privacy when their parents have none? No, that is my own little temple. It is where Ellie and I meditate and where I make my offerings to the new day."

Hilary was intrigued. This was a side to McConnel she would never have dreamed existed.

"Mind if I have a look?"

Gesturing wearily with one hand, he closed his eyes. Hilary pulled the curtain aside and moved behind it while Maddox stood above the prostrate hippy, gazing down with an enigmatic expression on his face. Since leaving the hospital he hadn't uttered a word and Hilary wondered what thoughts were going through his mind. He certainly hadn't shown any concern at the prospect of meeting the man he had beaten up and neither was there anything hostile in his manner, either to McConnel or herself. Shrugging inwardly, she left them to it and entered McConnel's temple.

Behind the curtain was a tiny little alcove. In stark contrast to the rest of the bus, it was spotlessly clean and showed signs of much caring attention. The floor was covered with rush matting and there were clean curtains on the tiny window. Shelves had been set up and an incense lamp burned brightly on one of these, its flame illuminating the picture of a multi-limbed Indian Deity. Another framed print depicted a pair of darkly hypnotic eyes above a purple yashmak and fresh greenery was arrayed around a small altar in one corner. Two small cushions had been placed side by side in the centre of the floor and in spite of its simplicity and the squalid surroundings, the little temple had an atmosphere of deep spirituality about it that stirred Hilary deep within her being. With a feeling of abandoning something very precious, she replaced the curtain and moved back toward the group around McConnel's bed.

"Don't you want to sit down?"

Ellie's tone made it obvious that she hoped they did not.

"Where?" Maddox broke his silence with a growl and Hilary couldn't help smiling. She remembered her own discomfort the previous night and the big fellow certainly had a point. There were no chairs in the bus, but Ellie gestured toward a battered bunk propped precariously against one wall.

"Visitors normally sit on that. It might be strong enough I suppose."

Maddox lowered his bulk suspiciously on to the flimsy bed while Hilary moved towards McConnel. Squatting on the floor beside him, she was suddenly very aware of his bare torso and the fact that from where he lay, he must have an excellent view of her stockinged thighs. Even as she realised this, the sudden glint in his eye confirmed her suspicions but she made no effort to move away.

Surprised at herself, she spoke hurriedly and inconsequentially.

"Tell me about your meditation, McConnel. What do you do?"

"I thought you came here to question me on the assault?" He mumbled and for a moment she was confused. "Still, never mind – I really don't want anything done about that. I will sort the matter out myself."

His eyes were momentarily very hard as he glanced at Maddox, but softened immediately when they came back to Hilary.

"I meditate for at least half an hour every morning and evening." He went on slowly, the lines of his face tense as he struggled to get the words out. "Ellie joins me when she feels like it and I find that it cleans my mind and makes every day seem worthwhile."

"How do you do it? I mean… what do you think about when you meditate?"

For a long moment McConnel gazed at Hilary, his eyes curious as though he was gauging whether her question was a genuine one or she was feigning interest in some obscure quest of her own. For her part, Hilary found herself almost transfixed by the strange green eyes, then his battered face contorted into a painful smile and he reached out slowly to put one grimy hand on hers.

59

Instinctively she tensed at his touch but made no move to pull away. She could feel the hard calluses on his palm and for a long, thoughtful moment, she was not even aware of the silent onlookers – PC Jeff Maddox and Ellie.

"You should try it Sergeant," his voice seemed stronger now. "It really is good for the body and the soul. We all have different ways to meditate but what I do is sit in the lotus position, clear my mind of all thought and work on the mantras. My favourite involves repetition of fractions and is quite complicated, but there are any number of routines one can go through."

"My sister thinks of colours," she told him. "She also meditates every day and she concentrates on particular colours in some sort of recognised sequence and apparently it not only makes her sleep well, but keeps her feeling good as well."

"Yes, I occasionally use the colour progression as well. As I said, Sergeant Bedwell, there are all sorts of routines to suit the individual and you really should give it a go. You have no idea of how much it will benefit you."

He looked deep into her eyes and for a long moment, the two of them were alone, the others forgotten and their respective positions and status in Society totally irrelevant. They were just a man and a woman together. A deep current of feeling passed between them and they were both terribly conscious of it.

The moment was very real to both of them but Hilary made a determined effort to break the spell. Yet even when she had taken a deep breath and pulled herself together, both she and McConnel were very aware that something had happened. Something that had no logic or sense of normality about it. Something that was somehow bigger than either of them and terribly difficult to understand.

McConnel spoke quietly and his words had nothing to do with that special moment of communion.

"There are so many ways of communicating with one's soul, Sergeant and we each have our own particular favourite. Your sister's colours will do for her what my fractions do for me."

He shook his head as though to clear it and Hilary understood exactly what he was feeling.

"Every morning, I greet the new day and offer it to Rama." He went on and suddenly his mind seemed to be drifting. "Ellie and I have a little ceremony in the temple and I make a symbolic offering of fire, water, earth and air – the ingredients of life itself. That is meant to ensure that the fates are kind to us in the hours ahead – although it is impossible to allow for the violence that is inherent in some human beings."

He glanced at Maddox and once again his eyes were horrifyingly pale.

"Once a year, my Indian teacher, Guru Dev pays our little ashram a visit and gives us a bit of instruction. When he is here, we hold the daily purifying service in the cottage where he stays."

"Ashram?"

"It is a traditional word for a commune or band of people who have renounced the world and live together in prayer and meditation. The Guru's spirit is always with us, even when he is on the other side of the world."

"Tell me about him, McConnel. Who is Guru Dev and where does he come from?"

Almost irritably, he shook his head again.

"Not now, Sergeant Hilary. Perhaps we will have a chance to talk about him some day. Suffice it to say that Guru Dev is a genuinely good man and there are few such left in this rotten world of ours."

There was a wealth of bitterness behind the softly spoken words and Hilary wondered what had brought on the sudden change of mood. Almost guiltily, she rose to her feet and she didn't miss the flash of disappointment in his eyes. It gave her a warm, wanted feeling in the pit of her stomach.

"We must go, McConnel." Her tone was brisk. "I will tell the medical people that you are okay, but I honestly do think you ought to go back for a check up in a day or two. Concussion can be dangerous you know and it tends to creep up on you if you aren't careful."

"Only if you drive me, Sergeant." The bantering tone was back and Hilary felt herself blushing. A little to her own surprise, she heard herself agreeing.

"I can't promise McConnel but I will see what I can do. Perhaps PC Maddox here can take you. I am sure you must have a great deal to talk about."

She knew she sounded waspish and glanced almost apologetically across at Maddox, but a little to her surprise, he treated the matter quite seriously.

"I'll be glad to, Sarge" he said heavily. "As you say, Scumbag and I are almost old friends now – know what I mean?"

"Don't call him that, you fat pig." Ellie burst out and moved threateningly toward the big policeman. Maddox held both hands up in surprised apology.

"Back off Girl. I didn't mean any harm. You people must surely be used to being called names?"

"Yeah, right. We are an' all: that's all people like you can do." She spat at him. "You don't understand us so you push us around and treat us like animals, but you can't come into my home and insult us like that. We 'ave the same rights as anyone else an' you knows it."

"She's right, Jeff." Hilary said quietly. "Come on, there's nothing more we can do here, so drive me back to the nick please."

Rising to his feet, Maddox grinned down at the battered looking man on the bed and when he spoke, his tone was almost friendly.

"Let me know when you need anything, Arsehole and I'll lay on the red carpet like – know what I mean?"

McConnel wordlessly waved him away and the two officers left the bus in silence. Hilary turned at the door and McConnel raised a hand in silent farewell. She looked hard at him before raising her own hand with a brief smile. Then she stepped into the sunlight, firmly closing the door behind her. Moments later it opened and Ellie stood in the doorway, watching them walk to the vehicle with her eyes narrowed and an unhappy expression on her face. When she returned to the prostrate McConnel, her mouth was set in tight lines of bitterness.

***

"You aren't going to make a fool of yourself with this toe rag are you, Sarge?"

Maddox asked the question quietly as he drove back toward the town and sensing Hilary's sharp glance across the vehicle at him, he held up a placating hand.

"I know; I know – it is none of my business, but listen to me a moment please."

He pulled the police car into a lay by, switched off the engine and turned in his seat towards her. Hilary waited grimly for what he had to say.

"You and I haven't always got on and that is probably my fault more than yours." The big man spoke quietly, but his voice was hard. "I don't like rankers at the best of times and when they are jumped up little girls, barely out of nappies who are pushed up above better coppers, I particularly don't enjoy them. No Sarge – hear me out please."

He held up a big hand again as she was about to explode with wrathful indignation and somewhat reluctantly, Hilary subsided into silence.

"I have probably given you a bit of a hard time over the past couple of months and perhaps I whacked that toe rag back there a little too hard, but he knows the score and I reckon he deserved what he got – know what I mean?"

For a moment, Hilary looked triumphant and opened her mouth to seize the opportunity, but Maddox cut her short.

"Oh yes Skip, I'll admit to giving him a bit of a going over, but you could never prove it. This conversation is between us and we don't have any witnesses to back you up, whereas I could probably produce three to confirm that I am not here. You know the score by now and so does McConnel. He took his knocks well and as I say, perhaps I was a bit hard on him, but that's all over now.

'But you, Sergeant Hilary Bloody Bedwell are my skipper and I do not want to see you land up in trouble – know what I mean? McConnel is a waster and nothing but strife. Hell Woman, we've both seen his type too many times before. He's a bit better educated than the average crusty and that seems to have struck a chord with you, but it is never worth it. Forget all about the bastard, Sarge and think about the job.

'You are on your way to the top Sergeant Bedwell and I want to be able to tell my grandchildren that I once worked with the first woman Commissioner of the Met – know what I mean? I don't want to see your career go down the pan for a fucking crusty."

Hilary smiled, but her lips were tight and her cheeks burned hotly.

"Don't you think you are stepping out of line, PC Maddox? I could have you for insubordination you know."

The big man laughed shortly.

"Come off it Lass. I was pounding the pavements while you were still in bloody nappies. Sure, you could call me up before the Guv'nor, but I would deny everything and it wouldn't reflect too well on you now, would it?

'No, as I said, this is strictly between you and me. We ought to be working well together you and I, not squabbling between ourselves – know what I mean?"

Easing himself around in the seat, he stared pensively at the road ahead.

"Let's call a truce between us, Sarge. For all your smarmy ways, I reckon you'll make a good copper if you stick to the straight and narrow and I'm prepared to help you go right up to the top. I can teach you all the tricks that are not found in Moriarty, but you'll have to promise me you will stick to concentrating on promotion.

'After all," he grinned sourly at her, "once you are made up, you'll move on and that will get you out of my hair so that life can get back to normal – know what I mean?"

"You mean I work you too hard, PC Maddox?"

Hilary couldn't help laughing at the big man and knew that he had a point and probably did have her welfare at heart. He was right too. She was making a fool of herself and ought to be concentrating on her career, not chasing after McConnel like a stage struck schoolgirl. Besides, having a man like Maddox in her corner could be of enormous assistance in the battle for promotion. With twenty-six years service behind him, he was a copper of the old school and could guide her through all the little pitfalls that lurked in wait for the aspiring senior officer.

After a moment of hesitation, she stuck out a hand.

"Okay Jeff – a truce it shall be. Now let's get back to the nick and wrap ourselves around a cup of tea and a very large sarnie."

"Willco Ma'am," He snapped her a mock salute and they drove on, both of them in a considerably better frame of mind.

***

For McConnel it was not so easy. As soon as the police car was out of sight, Ellie stormed back inside the bus.

"Wot is goin' on between you and 'er, McConnel?" She demanded. "I could see the way she was lookin' at you an' you with that stupid look on yore face too."

He sighed theatrically.

"Don't be daft Woman. She is a copper, not one of us. Sure she is a good looking piece, but we come from different worlds. How can she be interested in me, or vice versa for that matter. Life just doesn't work that way and you know it."

"All I know is there is something goin' on between you an 'er McConnel. I'm not stupid no matter wot you might think. I saw wiv my own eyes an' I'm tellin' you so."

The baby whimpered from the drawer they used as a cot and without another word, Ellie lifted it up in her arms and opened her dress to feed the child. At the sight of her small fat breast and engorged nipple, McConnel sighed again and closed his eyes. The situation was becoming ever more difficult and he was confused. He had felt that moment of communion with Hilary as keenly as she had and it had left him scarred and vulnerable, but longing to see her again. Yet none of it was practical. She had her life, he had his and there was absolutely no way in which the two could mix. There must inevitably be trouble if either of them attempted to cross the dividing line between them, yet the temptation to do so was incredibly strong. He wanted Hilary Bedwell. He needed Hilary Bedwell. The thought terrified him, but he knew that he was in love with Hilary Bedwell and the prospect of breaking off what little contact he had with her left him with a physical pain in his chest that was as bewildering as it was uncomfortable. Yet something had to be done or they were likely to destroy each other, as well as those closest to them.

"Do you want to move on?" He called across to Ellie, who sat with her back to him as she fed the baby. "We can make a fresh start somewhere else."

"No; I like it here and the kids are settled."

"It would save you getting your knickers in such a knot about Sergeant Bedwell." He pointed out mildly, but she didn't reply, so he closed his eyes again and tried to sleep.

But the man known only as McConnel was deeply troubled and sleep seemed submerged in a maelstrom of personal worries. He didn't care about Jeff Maddox or the beating he had received at the hands of the big policeman. Beatings were an occupational hazard of the life he had chosen and – without a word being spoken – he and Maddox had sorted out their differences as only two strong men can. There would be no more aggravation from PC Maddox, but the focus of McConnel's concern was Sergeant Hilary Bedwell.

The blonde policewoman was having far too much influence on his life and it wasn't due entirely to her good looks. Right from the start there had been a deep undercurrent of something different between them that belied their respective social standings and defied all logic. It was a feeling that needed to be sorted out one way or the other before it took over both their lives. Perhaps even ruined both their lives.

Groaning aloud at the thought, the bearded man shook his tousled head into the pillow and screwed his eyes tightly shut. From across the bus, Ellie saw and heard but made no comment. The baby sucked enthusiastically at her nipple and the dog raised its shaggy head to gaze with deep concern at the man who was its reason for being.

No matter how illogical it seemed, McConnel knew that his entire life had been irrevocably altered by that initial visit to The Beacon from Sergeant Hilary Bedwell.

CHAPTER SEVEN

She didn't see him at first. Hilary was patrolling the shopping centre on foot, enjoying the sunshine and the comfortable feeling of being in shirt sleeves for the first time that summer.

It was market day and the faces around her reflected the unexpectedly summery conditions. Weather-beaten farmers with collies at their heels, stopped to discuss stock prices with each other, brightly clad tourists photographed ancient buildings and mothers with toddlers in pushchairs talked shrilly about nothing in particular while keeping wary eyes on scampering toddlers. Shoppers hurried to get their chores done, while pigeons swooped with almost suicidal intent to rescue scraps of crisps or sandwiches left on the ground. Old men and women, worn out by a lifetime of toil, sunned themselves on handily placed benches while they watched the morning bustle. A busker wearing a jauntily tilted trilby strummed his battered guitar and sang with an enthusiastic lack of harmony, while the dog at his feet looked pleadingly at potential benefactors and in the doorway of a derelict shop, a young man who was obviously homeless stared listlessly out at the world.

It had been a lovely morning and there was a relaxed atmosphere in the town that was extremely pleasant. It was obvious that almost everyone was feeling good about life in general and many shoppers stopped to talk with the pretty police sergeant. Others contented themselves with smiling at her or calling greetings across the street. Her blonde hair shone in the sunshine and the rosy translucence of her cheeks made her look more like a pretty schoolgirl than a future police commissioner.

Hilary was listening patiently to the holiday reminiscences of a middle aged spinster, who had just returned from the Yorkshire Dales when she spotted the familiar woollen cap high above the heads thronging the little market. She had paid regular visits to the old red bus till McConnel was back on his feet, but it was nearly three weeks since she had seen the bearded hippy and his strange little family.

In those three weeks, Razor Wallace and his reluctant cronies had been released on bail by the local magistrates, Abie Whitehead had been committed to a higher court for trial and other matters of routine police interest had helped to take her mind off the strange feelings she had for McConnel.

It had not been easy to get him completely out of her thoughts though and in quieter moments, she found herself wondering where he was and what he was doing. Was he thinking of her or was he wrapped up in his life with that silly little Ellie?

A major part of Hilary's problem was that she had nobody she could speak to about McConnel. Her parents lived outside the county and anyway, she could not imagine their reaction if she visited them one day with McConnel in tow. Both the Bishop and her mother would be very polite as always, but inwardly they would be absolutely horrified and she would not want to put them through the inevitable trauma. A man like that was definitely not what they wanted for their eldest daughter and she knew how disappointed they would be if they knew of her burgeoning feelings for McConnel. She had one or two close friends who she could possibly discuss her dilemma with, but none of them lived nearby and a matter as personal as her lustful thoughts about one of society's misfits, was not something that could be talked about over a telephone.

In close proximity once more to that very same misfit, she could feel her heart beating faster with excitement. Unconsciously tucking an errant strand of hair back beneath her cap, she smiled across the heads at McConnel and felt herself sinking into the depths of those strange green eyes. The spinster's tales of walking in the hills were forgotten and after a searching look at the oblivious police officer, the lady flounced off, muttering under her breath about the rudeness of young people.

"Hello, Sergeant Bedwell." His deep, slow voice made her stomach tingle with reaction. He stood behind an open stall counter in the market and she stopped in front of him, looking sightlessly down at his wares. The counter was laden with coloured stones and shiny necklaces. Absently, Hilary fingered an egg-shaped rock, split neatly across its circumference and polished to a deep shine inside. She neither saw nor felt the stone in her hand and her eyes were fixed firmly on McConnel.

"It is called a thunder egg," he said softly. "They are only found on the beaches of Sri Lanka."

"What? Oh... I see... the stone. Yes, I was wondering where it came from."

"I could see that."

He was mocking her again and his eyes made her feel weak with a strangely exciting languor that threatened to throw her into his arms. Struggling to pull herself together, she changed the subject.

"How are the bruises, McConnel?"

Smiling gently, he fingered the skin above his eyes. The only visible sign of the beating he had received was a long white line below the tangled mass of his hair.

"I am alright now," he told her. "Still a bit creaky in the joints when the wind is blowing, but almost back to full fitness. Fancy a cup of coffee?"

"That would be nice. Can you leave all this or shall we take it with us?"

"That isn't a problem." He grinned at her. "Hold on a second and I'll arrange something."

Moving across to an adjoining stall, he talked quietly with a grey haired lady who was selling cheeses and she looked up somewhat incredulously at the police sergeant. Nodding vigorously, she obviously agreed to watch his stall while he was away and returning to Hilary's side, McConnel unselfconsciously took her arm.

They made an incongruous couple as they moved through the shoppers, their heads close together and their bodies almost touching at the shoulder. She the blonde, smartly dressed police officer, her shirt neatly pressed and her posture proudly erect, while he slouched along beside her – bearded, scruffy and wearing a grimy pullover in spite of the summer sunshine. A head taller than she was, he was forced to bend right down to hear her speaking and at one point, he put one dirty hand on her back in a gesture of agreement.

Chief Inspector Don Bolton was shopping with his wife on a rare day off when he spotted the oddly assorted couple.

"Well I'll be buggered!" He muttered coarsely to Mrs Bolton. "Will you take a gander at those two? What is that silly little woman up to now?"

"Perhaps it is business, Dear," she said a little doubtfully. "I know it doesn't look like that but perhaps he has asked her something."

"Or told her perhaps." The Chief Inspector mused. "That bloke must be this mysterious snout of hers and he has given her good stuff in the past.

'Here Love, let's walk down past them. I want to see her reaction when she spots me."

But Hilary had no eyes for her superior officer. She probably would not have seen him at all had not Chief Inspector Bolton moved directly into her path.

"Good morning, Sergeant Bedwell," he rumbled ominously and she looked up with only minor recognition registering on her features.

"Oh, hello Sir. Lovely day isn't it?"

Her smile was distracted and almost immediately she turned back to the man at her side, her attention totally taken up with what he was saying. Chief Inspector Bolton shrugged in baffled wonder and moved to catch up with his wife, his expression reflecting his bemusement. He was a vastly experienced police officer Don Bolton, but the situation was totally beyond him. Turning his head for another look at his subordinate, he was in time to see her throw back her head and laugh aloud, the clean lines of her neck, smooth and delightful in her enthusiasm.

"Well I'll be buggered with a rusty blow torch," he varied the refrain with unoriginal vehemence. "I don't think the lass really gives a tuppeny damn."

Shaking his head in bewilderment, the Station Chief Inspector hurried to catch up with his wife.

***

"Why do you call yourself McConnel?"

They were sitting on opposite sides of a small table in one corner of an organic coffee shop. All the other tables were occupied with morning shoppers or holidaymakers, but neither Hilary nor her companion had eyes for anyone else.

"Because it is my name, Sergeant. Why else?"

His smile was as gently mocking as ever and his twinkling eyes made her stomach tingle with excitement. For the moment, she didn't notice his black-rimmed fingernails, his scruffy clothing or the fact that his tangled mop of hair had not been washed in a very long time.

"But why no Christian names?" She persisted, enjoying the deep cadences of his voice and willing him to keep talking.

He laughed aloud – a great, booming laugh that echoed around the room and caused other customers to glance across at their table, one or two doing a distinct double take at the oddly assorted couple.

"What would you do with Alexander Herbert?" He chuckled. "I grew up with those horrors and you can imagine what I went through at school. I was only too glad to jettison them at the first opportunity. I often wonder whether parents think of their children when they bestow these fancy names upon them.

'Besides, as I told you at our first meeting, we have no need for first names in our society. I no longer look on myself as a Christian anyway. I follow my own God and try to be at peace with my fellow men. Organised religion is often bigoted and biased, so I avoid it as much as I can."

"How can you say that, McConnel? What about your chapel and Guru Dev?"

He laughed again, amused delight on his face.

"You remembered Sergeant Hilary; what a pleasure. I thought that little conversation would have gone straight over your head. Anyway, the Guru is like me and worships the universe rather than any particular Deity. You must come up and meet him when next he visits. You will enjoy his company, I promise you."

Hilary nodded slowly, her eyes clouding as she wondered whether the opportunity would ever arise. Only the previous evening, she had made up her mind to pull herself together and forget all about this man. Now he was charming her to such an extent that she was even contemplating an unofficial visit to The Beacon to visit with his Guru. Unconsciously, she shook her head and the blonde hair bobbed around her neck.

Grinning slyly into his coffee mug, McConnel sipped at the brew. The slurping sound he made would normally have set Hilary's teeth on edge, but she hardly noticed it in her delight at being with this strange man. She knew she was being totally stupid but for the moment at least, she didn't care. She had seen the disapproval in Chief Inspector Bolton's face and knew that she was probably jeopardising her career, but there was absolutely nothing at all she could do about it. McConnel held her spellbound and she listened to his voice and looked into his eyes in total fascination.

"Tell me about yourself." She urged. "I know nothing at all about you."

"Exactly as it should always be, Sergeant." He derided gently. "No wonder the public have lost faith in you lot. If you were in any way interested, you would have found out all about me by now. For all you know I might be a big time villain on the run.

'In fact, I am sorely offended that you haven't bothered Sergeant Bedwell. I really thought we had something going between us."

For all the facetiousness of his tone, it held an underlying note of seriousness that made them both pause. He looked into her face and for a moment, his gaze was troubled. She stared into his eyes and felt herself swimming in their molten depths. She was lost and in spite of her doubts, she knew it.

"Is there, McConnel? Can there ever be for that matter? We come from opposite sides of the track remember."

"That isn't quite what…" He began then shook his head distractedly. "No, you are quite right; of course we do and there can never be anything between us. For all that, you ought to have found out my vices by now."

Suddenly there was an invisible barrier between them and they both knew it. It might have come from the underlying seriousness of his words or it might have been due to an unexpected sexual tension that was affecting both of them. In spite of their vastly different lifestyles, backgrounds and expectations, they were man and woman and each of them was suddenly excruciatingly aware of it. For a few moments, they sat in silence, then in unspoken agreement, finished their coffee and rose to leave the café.

Outside the sun was still shining, shop windows sparkled in the sunshine, hordes of busy shoppers still milled, apparently aimlessly on the pavements and the life of the town went on as usual. Even the pigeons still flapped uncaringly at their feet, but for Hilary, something had changed and she wasn't sure what. She felt curiously alert, elated and depressed – all at the same time. McConnel walked silently beside her and neither of them said another word until they were well away from the café. On the corner beside the market, they stopped simultaneously.

"Well, thanks for the coffee, McConnel," she said with a heartiness she was a long way from feeling. "That was fun and I enjoyed the break"

"We must do it again," he said but there was no enthusiasm in his voice. Something had gone wrong between them and although each was aware of it, neither could have put a finger on what it was. For a long moment, they stood aimlessly, not looking at each other but reluctant to break off the contact between them.

They might have stood like that for some time, but their little cocoon of silent communication was suddenly shattered by the cataclysmic sound of an explosion somewhere nearby. Hilary was struggling to find suitable words of parting at the time and looking deep into McConnel's eyes. It seemed as though they were pools of calm water, suddenly broken up as a stone was cast into the centre of them. The emerald green depths seemed to fracture suddenly and the colours changed and changed again until his eyes were the harsh yellow topaz of a hunting cat. His entire body seemed to tense and for one long, broken second, he was not the man she had come to know. The scruffy, slouching reprobate gave way to a man of action, his movements athletic and alert. He whirled where he stood and she felt the electric tension in his body as he grabbed hold of her hand.

"That was a shot, Girl. A heavy revolver from the sound of it."

"Quick…"

Whatever she had been about to say was lost as a breathless young man skidded to a stop when he spotted her uniform.

"Help Officer – Sergeant;" the man gasped with a glance at her sleeve insignia. "There is trouble outside the building society and I think one of your lot has been shot."

Without another glance at McConnel, Hilary tore her hand free and began to run.

CHAPTER EIGHT

Jeff Maddox was conscious but only barely so. The bullet had smashed its way through the flesh of his thigh without breaking any bones, but material from his uniform trousers had been impacted into the wound. Although not life threatening, the resultant damage was extensive and sickening to look at.

The big policeman lay ashen-faced on the pavement, his head pillowed by a blanket and a pool of blood spreading rapidly below his lower body. An alarm bell clanged frantically and shocked onlookers moved hurriedly aside to make room for Hilary and her unusual companion, but she had no eyes for anyone other than the fallen policeman. Dropping to her knees on the pavement beside him, she heard her left stocking rip.

"Are you okay Jeff?" She asked the question automatically, then shook her head in disgust at herself. "No, sorry, of course you are not. The ambulance will be here in a moment and the paramedics will soon sort you out. I know it probably hurts like hell, but can you tell me what happened?"

Maddox tried to smile at her but his lips were taut and his eyes were clouded with pain. Hot bile rose to her throat as she looked down at the purple flesh surrounding his injury and in the ensuing silence, Hilary was suddenly aware of McConnel crouching beside her. Without any apparent haste, the bearded hippy seemed to take command of the situation and his presence gave the young policewoman a strange sense of comfort. After a brief look at the injured leg, he raised his head to the bystanders.

"I need a first aid kit – fast. There must be a chemist near here. And someone get that damned bell turned off please."

He spoke in flat, unemotional tones and two people immediately broke away from the group to run in different directions. Turning back to the injured officer, McConnel winced at the extent of the damage to the man's leg. Blood welled continuously from the wound and McConnel knew that if it wasn't stopped as a matter or urgency, the big fellow would die. It was as simple as that. Already, the colour had drained from his face and his lips were blue. His chances of survival were ebbing by the moment.

"You're sure that ambulance is coming?" He spoke quietly to Hilary from the side of his mouth and she made an effort to look away from Maddox' injuries and get a hold of herself.

"I'll check," she said briskly and took the personal radio from her belt.

"Control, control; this is Sergeant Bedwell. Do you read me, over?"

"Sergeant Bedwell, Control; go ahead Sarge."

While she spoke tonelessly into the set, McConnel put his hands deep into Jeff Maddox' mangled leg and for a moment, his body trembled as memories flooded through his mind.

Memories of other bodies, other bullet wounds. Memories of torn, purpled flesh and gaping rents that oozed or spurted blood, pus and spent cordite powder. Memories of shocked eyes and blank, pallid faces, already numbed with the inevitability of death. He remembered the coppery smell of fresh blood and the acrid taint of gunpowder. All too vividly, he resurrected the horror of flesh so scorched that it resembled nothing more than overdone roast meat.

The horrific memories brought sudden tears to his eyes and with them came the almost forgotten nightmares of personal involvement. The nightmares that had led him into an abrupt change of lifestyle – a change that had been nothing more than a desperate effort to escape the never ending treadmill of murder, arson, knee capping and beating. An effort to forget the shocked faces of survivors and the tears of grieving relatives. To forget the awful dangers and the hypocritical platitudes of politicians, senior officers and others who ought to have known better and cared not one jot.

All of it – the violence, the grief and the hypocrisy – had been the inevitable result of terribly troubled times, but he had thought those times were well behind him. He had seen it all, had lived through it all and had thought never to experience such horrors again.

But there could be no escape for men such as McConnel. His past was part of his present and the weakening groans of the injured policeman served only to emphasise the fact. Fumbling in the dreadful wound for the source of bleeding, he closed his eyes against the memories and a deep and painful shudder rocked his body. He worked like an automaton but his mind was elsewhere.

"These bastards used soft nosed ammunition," he told Hilary tonelessly. "See how the bullet has fragmented in his flesh and torn all the tissue around the entry hole? I'm not sure where the blood is coming from, but the femoral artery must be intact or he would have gone by now."

The alarm bell stopped with startling suddenness and around them the silence seemed deafening for the contrast with what had gone before. Having recovered somewhat from her initial shocked paralysis, Hilary glanced at her companion and was surprised to see that although his face was pale beneath the tangled beard, his hands were working with brisk, unhurried competence. His fingers were clamped in the messy flesh of Maddox' thigh as he worked to stop the pumping flow of blood. Somebody passed him a white first aid box and he grunted his thanks before gesturing to Hilary.

"The bleeding seems to have stopped but I don't want to let go for a moment or two. Open that lot up, Sergeant and let's see what we have to play with."

There was a note of natural command in his voice and Hilary meekly did as she was told, wondering a little at how McConnel had taken charge of the situation and how natural it seemed. At his bidding, she passed him a vial of antiseptic powder and a bundle of bandages, both triangular and crepe. Taking bloody fingers from the depths of the police officer's thigh, he watched for a moment to ensure that the bleeding didn't restart. Obviously satisfied, he glanced around him as though looking for something, then felt for Maddox' truncheon, tucked away in the specially constructed trouser pocket. His voice was calm when he spoke.

"Do you have one too?"

She nodded and produced her extendable baton. It was only nine inches long and much lighter than the old fashioned one, still carried by Maddox and a few of the older officers. McConnel looked at it briefly and pursed his lips, but didn't seem too concerned by the difference in weight and size between the two. Using the truncheons and bandages, he fashioned a makeshift splint on Maddox' leg. The big policeman was barely conscious and in obvious pain. Turning his chalky-white face restlessly from side to side, he groaned aloud while sweat ran down his cheeks in streams. Apart from the occasional glance to check on his condition, McConnel worked with brisk efficiency, shutting his ears to the big man's pain.

"The wound is not as bad as it might have been, but where is that bloody ambulance?" He gritted to Hilary at one stage. "Surely they should be here by now? At this juncture, speed is vital or he might well lose that leg."

"They should be here any minute now."

She automatically glanced at her watch, but even as she spoke, they heard the wail of a siren coming closer by the moment. By the time the vehicle slammed to a halt beside the grim little pavement tableau, Jeff Maddox' upper leg was neatly cocooned in white bandage. The bevelled ends of two black truncheons contrasted starkly with the snowy white material and McConnel sat wearily back on his haunches and watched the paramedics approach. Hilary Bedwell stood up to clear a path through the assembled bystanders so that the ambulance men could get through to PC Maddox.

The man in charge was the same one Hilary had rounded on when McConnel himself had been injured and he greeted the policewoman with an abashed smile. His eyebrows nearly disappeared into his cap when he spotted McConnel.

"You again," he muttered but McConnel was still in charge.

"Gunshot wound to the upper leg," he said quietly. "No bones broken. The bleeding has stopped for the moment and the femoral artery feels damaged rather than torn apart, which is a help. However, he lost a great deal of blood before we arrived on the scene and will need an immediate plasma infusion to cushion the shock. I would suggest you radio ahead for transfusions and immediate surgery to be made available or he will lose the leg. He really doesn't have much time."

Looking stunned and somewhat bewildered by the forcefulness of the scruffy young man, the medic issued crisp instructions to his colleagues, then crouched beside McConnel and the prostrate police officer. Having made a swift examination, he turned with evident curiosity to McConnel.

"You've done a pretty good job here, Mate and all we can really do now is give him a spot of morphine to ease the pain before we whip him off to casualty. Where did you learn your first aid?"

Ignoring the question, McConnel rose slowly to his feet and stretched his arms above his head to ease the tension in his muscles. His face was very pale above the matted beard and the look in his eyes was bleak. He watched blankly as Maddox was loaded into the ambulance and as the vehicle howled away, he looked at the people around him. Hilary didn't think he was seeing a thing.

"Tonto will be alright I reckon." He muttered tonelessly and she smiled in obvious relief. "Do we know what happened yet?"

Hilary nodded grimly.

"It seems that two men walked into the building society, a firearm was produced and they walked off with a load of cash. Jeff was passing by, realised something was amiss and tried to intervene. They shot him and escaped in a red Sierra. He had the presence of mind to take the number even though he was badly hurt and hopefully, they will be picked up before too long."

She spoke simply and the words sent another shudder through McConnel's body. More memories surged through his sub conscious. Memories of other young men and women facing violent death with a calm insouciance that defied all logic. Men and women who walked into all sorts of dangerous situations merely because it was their duty to do so. Men and women whose calm heroism was seldom recognised and rarely appreciated by the public they served.

Just as Jeff Maddox had done his duty and been shot, it could as easily have been the girl at his side. Had she not been with him, Hilary Bedwell might well have been the one to disturb the fleeing gunmen. It might have been Hilary lying on the pavement, her leg shattered or her life ebbing away with her blood on the concrete paving stones. The thought made him feel sick and for a moment, his legs buckled and his already pale skin seemed to whiten even further.

"Are you okay?"

Hilary peered up into his face and he made a visible effort to pull himself together. Taking a deep breath and swallowing hard, he nodded slowly without answering the question. Pulling a filthy handkerchief from a pocket of his jacket, he wiped sweat from his forehead and tried to smile, although his eyes were troubled.

"Just a bit of reaction I suppose. I'm fine now."

"You were wonderful," she told him with quiet enthusiasm. "I don't know where you learned your first aid McConnel, but I would have been in a fine old pickle if you hadn't been with me. I don't know how I can possibly…"

He cut her off with a smile and gestured to the street behind her.

"You would have coped just as well without me, Sergeant Bedwell, so let's forget it. Here comes the cavalry so you had better be properly official while I quietly disappear."

She turned to see Chief Inspector Bolton, Detective Inspector Hollis and a couple of CID aides leaping out of a traffic car and hurrying toward the scene. The burly officer in charge was still in his shopping clothes and looked very hot under the collar. He frowned when he spotted Hilary and her companion.

"Ah Sergeant Bedwell," he began officiously, "perhaps you can tell me what is going on? I have only had garbled reports so far and I am becoming more confused by the moment. Is it true that Jeff Maddox has been shot?"

"True enough I'm afraid Sir."

She brought him and the detectives up to date with a brisk summary of what had taken place and all four men listened attentively. The DI frowned heavily and his two aides looked serious, but Don Bolton was obviously impressed by her grasp of the situation and the concise manner in which she summarised it.

"Do we know who these villains were, Sergeant?" DI Hollis put in. "Did PC Maddox have a chance to see their faces?"

"I'm not sure Sir, because although he gave me the vehicle number, he was in a lot of pain and I didn't press him too much for details. In fact, if it hadn't been…"

She turned to include McConnel in the conversation, but true to his word, the hippy had slipped away through the crowd and was nowhere to be seen. With a feeling of genuine disappointment, she turned back to her boss and the other police officers.

"If it hadn't been for what, Sergeant?"

With a sigh of resignation, Hilary shook her head.

"Nothing, Sir. I had better be getting back to the nick though. There will be a lot to do after this one."

CHAPTER NINE

Hilary sat demurely in front of her irascible boss. It was three days since the shooting and Chief Inspector Bolton was back in full regalia, his tunic neatly pressed and a starched shirt collar tight around his massive neck. His attitude towards the blonde sergeant was still somewhat formal, but definitely more relaxed than it had been on the occasion of her last visit to his office.

"You will be pleased to know that Jeff Maddox is going to make a full recovery, Sergeant." He told her briskly. "I've just had Doctor Jones on the blower and she was fulsome in her praise for the repair job you did on Jeff's leg. Without your help, he would almost certainly have lost the limb altogether and might well have fallen off his perch through loss of blood."

"I had very little to do with it, Sir," Hilary shook her head. "I merely watched while McConnel did the work. I wouldn't have known where to start with an injury like that and while I was dithering, McConnel seemed to just take over. He was the one who saved PC Maddox' life, not me."

For a moment, the big Chief Inspector looked almost apoplectic.

"McConnel, Sergeant? Do you mean that low life I saw you canoodling with in the High Street shortly before the shooting?"

"McConnel is a long way from being a low life and I was NOT canoodling with him, Sir." Hilary could feel her cheeks flushing and made an effort to speak as levelly as possible. "I had a cup of coffee with him and we were talking together when PC Maddox was shot in the next street. He was a huge help at the scene and if anyone saved PC Maddox' life, it was McConnel, not me."

Chief Inspector Bolton shook his head in disgusted impotence.

"Well, anyway Sergeant; one or other of you definitely did a bloody good job in patching up Jeff Maddox. I am not sure what is going on with that crusty of yours, but I intend to find out and then we could be having words again and they might not be pleasant. However, in the meantime you can tell your friend that he saved my officer's life and will be entitled to some sort of reward from County Headquarters."

"There's irony for you," Hilary murmured under her breath and wouldn't elaborate when Bolton asked her what she meant.

"It is nothing, Sir. Just a private thought. McConnel won't accept anything Sir. I am quite sure of that. He just isn't the type."

"I am sure you know him better than most, Sergeant," Bolton's tone was dry. "When or if you see him, please convey my thanks and tell him about the possible reward."

"Yes of course, Sir. What is happening about the villains who shot PC Maddox? Are we any closer to finding out who they were?"

In spite of county wide roadblocks and extensive house to house enquiries, the red Sierra had not been found and after two days, the chase seemed to have gone cold. Bolton smiled enthusiastically at her question though.

"The 'suits' had a bit of a break through yesterday." He told her cheerfully. "One of the witnesses remembered hearing a gang member refer to their leader as 'Raze' and in spite of the stocking masks, the description tallies with our old friend Razor Wallace. There is an all points warning out on him and those two young yobbos who were in the drug deal with him. It shouldn't take too long to pick them all up.

'Jeff himself is still too weak to say much, but we are hoping he will give us a positive ID when he is back to normal."

"How long is he likely to be out of action, Sir?"

Bolton allowed himself another smile and Hilary reflected that he seemed extremely pleased with himself.

"Thanks to you Sergeant – and the dropout of course…"

"McConnel." She reminded gently and he looked confused for a moment.

"Ah yes, McConnel. Yes well, thanks to you and your McConnel, he should be back on light duties in about four weeks, provided he isn't too buggered emotionally to get on with the job. I suppose counselling will be laid on if he wants it, but…"

"Not Jeff Maddox, Sir. He is an old timer and will sort himself out without any help from the shrinks. If I know Jeff at all, he will be only too keen to get back, even for light duties."

"My feelings exactly, Sergeant Bedwell. The sooner we have Jeff back in harness and those three villains behind bars, the better it will be for all of us.

'Do you know," his tone became quite conversational; "that they did a four hour op on Jeff's leg and fitted all the pieces back together like a bloody jig saw. Amazing what they can do these days hey? When I was a lad, they would have lopped the whole thing off and fitted him out with a walking stick."

"Have we any idea where Wallace is likely to be?"

Hilary brought her boss back to more mundane matters and he shook his head.

"No, I'm afraid the little bastard has gone to ground and for the moment, nobody knows where. I don't suppose it will take long for the word to spread around his usual haunts though and he will come soon enough. Villains don't like it when a copper gets shot. It gives them all a bad name and causes far too much fuss and palaver in their lives."

Ten minutes later, Hilary left the Chief Inspector's office, her head still ringing with his praises. She couldn't help a wry smile as she compared her feelings with the way they had been on the last occasion she had emerged from that particular room. Hurrying down the corridor to her own office, she took a sheet of paper from a drawer and began scribbling down notes for her report on the first aid treatment given to PC Jeff Maddox. She was determined that McConnel should have some sort of official recognition for saving the big constable's life and knew that she had to get her word in first or his efforts would quickly be forgotten or ignored.

As a police officer, Hilary Bedwell was possessed of an almost frightening single mindedness. Among her colleagues it had long been recognised that she could concentrate on a given subject, no matter what was going on around her at the time. It was a talent that had always stood her in good stead, yet suddenly it seemed to have deserted her.

It wasn't that there were any obvious distractions to interrupt her thought processes. She was alone in the office and the rest of the station had the normal morning hum of any busy offices. No, it was just that her brain kept drifting back to McConnel, his incredibly capable handling of Jeff Maddox' injuries and his abrupt disappearance when others had appeared on the scene. That had been a disappointment, as she would have enjoyed the look on her senior colleagues' faces when she had told them of his handiwork.

She had so enjoyed the morning too. For all his scruffy appearance and somewhat gamey smell, McConnel had been fun to be with and while their shared coffee had been overshadowed by the violent events that followed, every word he had said still burned in her mind. She could picture the self-mocking glint in his green eyes when he spoke about himself and remembered the deep timbre of his voice and the soft smile that hovered about his shaggy lips.

She remembered too her own amazement at the calm efficiency with which he handled the awful wound to Jeff Maddox' leg and wondered more than ever about his past life. Where had he come from? His cultured way of speaking marked him down as something more than the ordinary drop out or traveller and where on earth had he gained his medical expertise – and expertise it certainly was. No common or garden first aider could have coped so efficiently with that awful hole in the policeman's thigh. There weren't even too many trained police officers who could have done such a professional job of cleaning out and bandaging the injured leg. McConnel had obviously done that sort of thing before, but where and how was it possible? Why would a man with such obvious skill be wasting his life in a hippy commune?

None of it made sense and coming to a sudden decision, Hilary jumped up from her desk, took the area car keys from their hook in the Control Room and hurried out to the police garage.

"I'll be on the air if you need me for anything." She said shortly to her fellow sergeant on duty, who was loitering behind a pretty radio operator. "Shouldn't be more than forty minutes."

Looking grimly determined, Hilary Bedwell drove out of town and made for the little community on the hill known as Swanwick Beacon. She was going to solve the enigma that was McConnel for once and for all.

***

"I'm tellin' you, Sergeant B, I dunno where 'e is. None of us 'as seen 'im for days like. 'E just 'asn't come 'ome since that copper was shot. Do you think 'e 'ad anyfing to do with that?"

The speaker was Ellie and they were standing just inside the old red bus. Hilary looked at the girl with concern. Ellie could never have been called a beauty, but she had obviously been crying a great deal and her face was puffed and discoloured, the general effect making her look like an overweight chicken, hastily prepared for the dining table. Although she felt naturally sorry for the girl, Hilary couldn't help wondering again what

McConnel saw in her. Banishing the bitchy thought with an effort, Hilary concentrated on the reason for her visit.

"No Child, he definitely wasn't involved. He was with… Anyway, just take it from me that he had nothing whatsoever to do with the shooting."

She couldn't have explained even to herself why she should be so hesitant to say that she and McConnel had been together, but the thought of admitting it to McConnel's partner whoever she might be, seemed somehow uncomfortable. A little to her own amazement, Hilary felt a deep sense of guilt about being with Ellie's man, even for an innocent cup of coffee.

"I don't suppose there is anything wrong, Ellie." She went on soothingly. "He probably wants to get away from all the fuss. He really was quite a hero at that bank scene you know."

"I know Sergeant B. The others 'ave been full of it, but I just wish 'e'd come back to tell me 'isself."

"Has he ever stayed away like this before?"

The girl nodded and more tears sprang to her eyes.

"'E sometimes goes off in the woods by 'isself to meditate and then 'e loses all track of time like. But even then, the longest 'e 'as stayed away is a day or so. I 'aven't seen 'im now for four days an' I'm worried sick."

In spite of her deep-seated antipathy toward McConnel's woman, Hilary felt her heart go out to her. Stepping forward, she put her arm around bony shoulders and Ellie immediately collapsed against her and burst into anguished sobbing.

"When I 'eard there'd bin a shooting in town and McConnel was involved, I thought 'e might 'ave done it see, Sergeant B. I've never knowd 'im to be tooled up, but I was scared 'e might 'ave been shot 'isself or arrested like. I 'aven't slept since 'e left an' the kids 'ave been all fretful like too."

Hilary hastened to reassure the weeping girl, but wasn't sure that her words were even getting through to Ellie.

"He was the hero of that shooting Ellie, I can tell you. Without McConnel there to sort things out, PC Maddox would probably have lost his leg or perhaps even his life. Your man was a star Girl and I am personally going to recommend that he gets a reward for his actions. Believe me, he deserves a medal."

"'E won't take it, Sergeant B. I know 'im too well and he ain't interested in anyfing like that. Besides 'e 'as plenty of 'em and wot good do they do 'im?"

"Plenty of what, Ellie?"

Hilary was suddenly curious, but Ellie merely shrugged.

"Medals like: 'E was pissed and showed 'em to me once, but I dunno where 'e keeps 'em or even if 'e still 'as 'em. 'E's a real mystery man is McConnel but I can tell you for a fact that 'e won't accept any reward."

Yet again, Hilary felt an unreasoning stab of jealousy at the girl's intimate knowledge of McConnel. Struggling to keep her feelings in check, she looked earnestly into the pinched face and used her own handkerchief to wipe Ellie's dribbling nose.

"We will worry about that when the time comes, Ellie." she soothed. "For now, our main priority must be to find McConnel."

"'E's a good man, Sergeant B," the girl said inconsequentially, grabbing Hilary's hands in hers as she did so. "'E looks after us so well, even though 'e 'as never really bin one of us like. Not proply any'ow. I've always been scared of 'im leaving for good and now 'e's gone and done it see.

'Oh but I wish 'e would come back."

The last few words came out in a wail and Hilary absently patted her shoulder. In her own mind, she was wondering why or how McConnel came to be in possession of medals and whether he had earned them – and if so, how – or whether they were stolen property of some sort.

"Where might he have gone, Ellie? I mean - where is his home? Where does he come from?"

"I dunno, Sergeant B. I've never 'eard 'im talk about 'is past life."

"How did he come to show you the medals then?"

"I dunno." She sniffed loudly and Hilary absently handed her the already sodden handkerchief. "'E was rantin about politicians or something and I don't remember why 'e got 'em out. I 'ave often tried to find out about 'is family an' all, but 'e just clams up and won't say anything when I ask like."

"When and where was he born?"

"I dunno." Her round face was twisted with anguish and tears flowed freely down her cheeks. "'E never once 'ad a birthday that I knowd of and once when I asked 'im, 'e didn't 'alf snap at me."

"Do you know how old he was then?" One look at the girl's blank expression answered the question and she went on before she got another 'dunno.' "No, I don't suppose you do if you can't even tell me his birthday."

Picking up her bag, she looked around to make sure she hadn't left anything behind while Ellie watched her numbly.

"I must go now, My Dear. Is there anything more I can do to help?"

The girl hesitated and seemed on the verge of saying something. Hilary paused in the doorway, her bag dangling from her fingers.

"Yes Ellie – what is it?"

"Just find 'im for me please Sergeant Hilary. Tell 'im we need 'im like – me and the kids can't do nuffin' without 'im Miss. 'E told me once that if anyfing ever 'appened to 'im…"

A noise behind her made Hilary turn and the moment was lost. The toddler stood just inside the door, still dressed in the grimy tee shirt and her big eyes fixed on the police sergeant. Her thumb was jammed into her mouth and she stood in total silence, her free hand buried in the neck fur of the big Alsatian. The dog also eyed Hilary with obvious interest. It held its shaggy head low and she wasn't sure whether the look in those amber eyes signified acceptance or hostility. Smiling somewhat hesitantly at the ill assorted duo, she turned back to Ellie.

"What did he tell you, Ellie?"

But whatever the girl had been about to say had gone. The sudden interruption had either driven it from Ellie's mind or given her time to consider her own interests in the matter. Whatever the case, it was obvious that she wasn't going to say more. She shook her head emphatically.

"Nuffin' Sergeant B. Just nuffin' at all like."

One look at her sullen expression told Hilary that it was no good pursuing the matter and she drove away from the Beacon feeling very dissatisfied with her own handling of the interview. She was still shaking her head in self-disgust when she arrived back at the police station.

***

McConnel sat in the darkness of the forest, his back against a tall oak tree. Six feet in front of him, the two hippies, Spike Moroney and Robbie Ellis sat on a fallen log, but their stiff and uncomfortable postures were in marked contrast to McConnel's languid informality. The smell of burning cannabis floated around the little group and seemed to hang like an uncomfortable cloud about their shoulders.

"What the fuck got into you, Spike?" It was rare for McConnel to use profanity and his companions were well aware of it. "Why try something on that scale, particularly when you were already in the shit over the gear? Now we have a copper shot and the ruddy world and his wife will be hunting you down."

"Razor reckoned it would be a doddle, McConnel." Spike whined ingratiatingly. "The bastard told us 'e 'ad cased the building society an' all we 'ad to do was go along for the ride an' a bit of support just in case things didn't go properly like. 'Ow was we to know 'e was carrying?"

"You are bloody fools to be taken in by that homicidal idiot." McConnel muttered grimly and both his listeners seem to cringe inwardly at his words. Although he was dressed as they were, smelled as bad as they did and was every bit as stoned as they were, there was something very different about McConnel and all three of them were aware of it. He was a natural leader of men and for years, the two younger hippies had been coming to him for advice and support when it was needed. Now it almost seemed as though by allying themselves with Razor Wallace and getting involved in the botched bank raid, they had somehow let him down and needed his forgiveness.

"The problem is," McConnel went on in abstract tones, "what are we going to do about it now?"

"There's a couple of vans going up north the day arter tomorrow." Robbie put in eagerly. "Per'aps we can join in wiv 'em and disappear like."

McConnel looked pained at the suggestion.

"For once in your benighted life, try not to be such a dickhead Robbie. The filth will have had you sussed out long since and any move you make, they will be on to you like flies on a week old turd.

'No," he shook his head emphatically; "there is only one thing for it, Fellas. You are going to have to give yourselves up."

"What?"

Moroney was genuinely horrified and the question came out as an indignant squawk. Gravely, McConnel held up a hand for silence.

"Hear me out, Fellas. It won't be as bad as all that. The filth know all about Razor Wallace and I'll bet he is already in the frame, which means that you two will be as well. On the other hand, they will also be aware that he is a different class of villain to you guys. If you make full confessions and put all the blame on him, then I reckon you should get off with probation at the most. It is Razor that the cops want to see behind bars. You two are small fry."

Neither of his listeners appeared convinced.

"It's orlrite for you like, McConnel." Spike told him sourly. "You won't be in the dock when time in the slammer is 'anded out. We are already in the frame for the drugs an' all, so the Beak is going to send us down as sure as hell."

"Okay, what else can you suggest?"

McConnel asked the question in reasonable tones, but even as he spoke, he thought of a possible answer and an unholy grin blossomed in the depths of his beard. For nearly a minute, there was silence in the forest as the other two watched him anxiously and when he did speak, there was an air of suppressed excitement in his voice that wasn't lost on his listeners.

"Just supposing Razor gave himself up, Fellas," he said slowly, "do you think he would grass on you two?"

"Never in a 'undred years like." Spike sounded confident but Robbie shook his head in disgust.

"Come off it McConnel. Razor ain't gonna do that now is 'e? 'E's an 'ard bastard, that bloke and the filth will have to get 'im bang to rights before they lock 'im up. I wouldn't be surprised if 'e don't give 'em a good fight too. Wiv a copper already down, 'e's got nuffink to lose like.

'No, Razor ain't gonna 'and 'imself in. That's crazy thinking, Man."

"Perhaps I can persuade him." McConnel was still smiling gently through his beard. "Even if I don't, what happens when the Old Bill nick him – as they will eventually? Will he squeal on you two fellas?"

Both men shook unkempt heads, Spike with confidence but Robbie considerably more hesitantly. McConnel leaned forward to speak again.

"Okay then, I will see Razor and see if I can persuade him to give himself up before you have to do it. Perhaps we can do some sort of a deal to keep your names out of it."

"But 'ow the fuck do you reckon to do that then?" Spike sounded anxious, but McConnel merely grinned at him.

"That you can leave to me, Spike. Let's just say that I will have a friendly chat with the bloke and I am sure we can come to some agreement.

'Where has he gone to ground?"

This time it was Spike who hesitated.

"We ain't supposed to know this McConnel an' if Razor thought we 'ad grassed 'im up, 'e'd do us in, I'm tellin' you. Like I say, 'e's a 'ard man that Razor an' I wouldn't want 'im to know it was me that let 'im down like."

"He won't know where I got it from." McConnel reassured him. "I have my own contacts, everyone knows that. Any of them could have told me about Razor. Besides, how on earth did you manage to find out where he is? I wouldn't have thought him likely to confide in you two."

The appeal to his vanity was too much for Spike and his eyes lit up as he recalled his moment of glory.

"It was dead simple like, I'm tellin' you now. Once that copper went down, we knew we was in trouble like. Razor told us before 'and that if there was strife, we would dump the motor and split up. It sounded easy like an' 'e promised to divvy up the loot in Jamesons' Caff the following day. Anyway, it all went like clockwork see. We left the motor on the edge of Rendford, then we all scarpered. Only I went the wrong way see an' when I turned a corner, there was Razor opening up an old garage. I yelled an' 'e looked sick when 'e saw me, but 'ad no choice but to let me dive inside like.

'That little gaff might look like an ordinary lock up from the outside, but it is all done up like a flat inside. All 'ome comforts and central 'eating an all, but you wouldn't know it from the street see. Tha' Razor, 'e's a crafty one, I'm tellin' you."

His story finished, Spike looked anxiously at McConnel who merely nodded soothingly.

"A crafty one indeed, Spike, but he has yet to deal with me. This drum of his, I suppose he keeps it for just such emergencies and it is well stocked with food and drink etcetera. Possibly even hot and cold running blondes in case his stay in there is a long one?"

Spike shook his head quite seriously and the other listened with interest.

"I dunno about the blondes like McConnel, but 'e's got it all kitted out see. There's everything 'e could possibly want in there, even a radio specially tuned to the cops' channel. They'll never catch 'im I'm tellin' you."

"We'll see." McConnel rejoined grimly. "Where did you say this palace of desires is – Orient Street?"

"Nah, it's down on Morton Road – be'ind number twenty-one like. It's an empty drum that used to belong to a copper who got transferred. Ow's that for a laugh then?"

"Very droll." McConnel agreed but there was little humour in his eyes. Razor Wallace seemed to have put an enormous spoke into the even tenor of McConnel's own existence and by shooting Jeff Maddox had effectively put paid to the budding friendship between McConnel and Sergeant Hilary Bedwell. Having seen him at work, she would be curious as to how he came by his expertise and he knew that with a little digging, she could find out a great deal about him. Things would never be the same between them and the thought brought an unaccustomed ache to the bearded hippie's heart.

It was time to move on, but McConnel bleakly determined that Razor Wallace was going to pay dearly for interfering so drastically with his life.

CHAPTER TEN

McConnel stood silently in the shadows, his eyes fixed on the garage door across the street. He had been in position for over four hours, but as yet there was no sign of his quarry.

Although he was dressed in his usual filthy attire and the bobble hat was still perched on top of his matted locks, there was a subtle change in McConnel's appearance. The difference did not lie with his clothing or his cleanliness. It was something far more difficult to define, something that had changed in his general demeanour and something not readily apparent even to the most experienced observer.

Gone was the slouching down-and-out that Hilary Bedwell found so strangely attractive. Gone was the quietly confident leader of the Beacon Community and gone was the competent medic who had saved the life and limb of PC Jeff Maddox. In place of all these different versions of the man known as McConnel was a desperately dangerous hunter, waiting with infinite patience for his quarry to come into view.

McConnel's body was held straight and tense, his muscles poised and ready for instant action. His eyes were clear and watchful, without the cannabis film that characterised the usual McConnel. He stood absolutely motionless and there was an air of menace about him that made him a curiously terrifying sight. If Hilary Bedwell had seen him at that moment, she might not even have recognised the man who had so unexpectedly come into her life.

But Hilary Bedwell wasn't there to see him and although McConnel thought of her with fierce longing, he knew that he had to concentrate on the task at hand. So it was that he stood with his back against a derelict building, waiting with all the patient menace of a jungle predator. He was a carnivore on the hunt and his unknowing quarry was Razor Wallace.

It was almost midnight before the door to the garage opened and Wallace's head appeared cautiously in the entrance. There was no light to give him away, but McConnel's eyes were rested and his night vision was acute. He waited with his senses concentrated on the man across the street and a small, mocking smile on his lips.

Scuttling furtively out of his garage, Wallace turned to lock the door behind him. The night was completely silent and he came very close to having a heart attack when a calloused hand closed over his mouth and an arm like a steel band clamped itself around his chest.

"Easy does it, Razor," McConnel whispered. "We don't want any trouble, do we and I certainly do not want to hurt you. Don't make a sound and let's move back inside before someone sees us, shall we?"

Without easing his grip from the suddenly frightened criminal's face, McConnel eased the door open with one foot and pushed Razor Wallace back into the garage. The darkness inside was absolute and for a moment, the two men stumbled together like a pair of awkward waltzers. McConnel felt his captive tense and tightened his grip around the man's chest.

"Don't do anything foolish now, Razor. As I said, I have no wish to hurt you. I am even going to let you go for a moment. I want you to relock the door and get some lights on in this place."

Once again, the muscles beneath his arm tensed in wary anticipation and McConnel continued with a warning note in his voice.

"I asked you not to be silly, Razor. I am stronger than you and can run considerably faster. Believe me, I won't be nearly so gentle if you give me any grief."

Carefully taking his hand away from the man's mouth, he heard Wallace gasp as he struggled to get his breath back. For the moment, McConnel kept his other arm firmly in place around Wallace's ribs and as the man struggled to regain his equilibrium, a slight tightening of the pressure served to warn him of the possible consequences, should he try to escape.

"Who… who the fuck are you?"

The breathless question seemed to reverberate around the silent room and McConnel squeezed again in warning.

"Keep it quiet please, Razor. We don't want to attract attention now, do we? In a little while, everything will be clear as day as far as you are concerned."

"You're not… not….not the fucking law then?"

McConnel chuckled quietly.

"No Razor, I am not the filth, although I am very much on their side at the moment. I am going to let you go now, so move very slowly and think hard on the possible consequences before you try anything foolish. Believe me, I really do not want to hurt you, but…"

The unfinished sentence was full of menace and Razor Wallace trembled in his fear.

Releasing his iron grip on Wallace's chest, McConnel pushed him away so as to keep his own arms free in case they were needed, but Wallace obviously had no intention of trying anything untoward. He had always boasted that he wasn't scared of any man, but he had felt the strength behind that crushing grip on his chest and didn't want to provoke his assailant into further violence. Besides, he was curious to see exactly who he was up against.

Moments later, the door was once again securely locked, an overhead light bulb came on and Razor Wallace turned slowly, his eyes screwed up against the glare.

Anticipating the moment, McConnel had put on a pair of dark glasses, but his appearance was unmistakable in spite of the shades.

"I know you." Wallace was clearly astonished. "You were in the Pheasant when the feds picked us up the other night. McConnell isn't it? What the fuck do you think you are doing now?"

With identification, his confidence returned with a rush. Hippies and travellers he could deal with and although he had never had anything to do with McConnel, he held him in the same contempt that he felt for Spike Moroney and the other scruffs.

For the moment, that vice-like grip around his ribs and his own palpitating fear were forgotten. He would deal with this interfering idiot and make him sorry that he had ever met Razor Wallace. He opened his mouth to speak, but McConnel held up a hand in warning. His quietly spoken words and an innate sense of survival made Wallace hold back the threats he had been intending to utter. "Don't be foolish now, Razor." McConnel warned in softly disdainful tones. "I am a peaceful soul, but if necessary I will beat you to a pulp and throw the lot into the nearest wheelie bin."

But Razor Wallace hadn't learned discretion. His fear had been replaced by a fierce embarrassment at having been bested by this scruffy drop out, who obviously couldn't have known who he was dealing with. After all, Razor Wallace had a reputation to uphold and this waste of oxygen wasn't going to spoil that. Spinning on his heel, he made for the door, his fright and his caution completely forgotten.

"I'm getting out of here, Arsehole," he grated. "I dunno what the fuck you're playing at, but I'm damned if I am going to be pushed around by a dirty fucking scumball like you."

"You are damned anyway I'm afraid," McConnel's tone was reasonableness itself. "Please don't make me do something I might regret Razor, there's a good chap."

But his polite plea was ignored. Forgetting caution in his need to escape, Razor Wallace took hold of the key in the door and began to turn it in the lock.

Showing no trace of undue haste, McConnel moved across the room in two long strides and before he had turned the key through even one revolution, Wallace found himself caught in the most excruciatingly painful grip he had ever experienced. Somehow McConnel had taken hold of his elbow and with almost unnoticed pressure from his fingers, made even the slightest movement an unbearable agony.

"Aaagh!"

Rising on his toes in an effort to escape the pain, Razor couldn't help crying out in his distress. Icy shafts of agony seemed to bore upwards into his brain and there was nothing he could do to lessen the torment."

"Oh Razor, Razor old chap, I did warn you. Why do people like you never listen to well meant advice? I had hoped to avoid this sort of unpleasantness."

"What do you want then?"

Wallace's voice was tight with pain and McConnel looked almost regretfully down into his face. The green eyes above the tangled beard held an expression of gentle concern.

"Only a little talk Razor. Don't you think it is time we chatted a while?"

Moving slowly, he propelled the moaning criminal into a chair, propped up in one corner of the room.

"Sit down," he advised and once the man was seated, McConnel released his grip and stood back, absently massaging his fingers.

"I want you to do something for me Razor old chap." He spoke in conversational tones. "I don't suppose you will like it, but I am sure I will be able to convince you eventually. It is up to you whether you agree quickly or I am forced to resort to more of those painful little moves, I have in my armoury. Mind you, my skills are getting a bit rusty and I do need the practice."

Razor Wallace looked up into McConnel's eyes and for once in his bullying life, he was truly afraid. The eyes no longer held any hint of mockery or good humour. The emerald green that had so turned the head of Sergeant Hilary Bedwell had disappeared and been replaced with a pale, flinty colour that seemed infinitely menacing. McConnel's eyes were the green of an Antarctic ice wall – cold, bleak and desperately dangerous. They were the eyes of a killer – the eyes of a snake that has its prey helpless in front of it. Razor looked into their depths and feared for his life. He felt his stomach curdle in his terror and when he spoke, his voice was a whimper.

"I'll give you anything you want, McConnel. I promise you. Just say the word man and I'll make you rich."

"I don't actually want anything Razor. My needs are few and you couldn't help me anyway." He spoke in gentle tones. "There is something I would like you to do for me though, so make yourself comfortable while I tell you about it."

***

"It is Thursday today and as we don't have a hell of a lot on, I want a concerted effort to collar Thursday Joe. If someone in this relief can nick him, it will be a feather in all our caps."

The speaker was Hilary Bedwell and she was briefing the members of her shift before they set out on their afternoon duties. She nodded and smiled at the hulk of a man, lolling in his chair at the back of the briefing room, two metal crutches propped against the wall beside him.

"I am sure you will all join me in welcoming Jeff Maddox back, although you will probably be as surprised as me at the speed of his recovery."

It was less than four weeks since the bank raid and Hilary had indeed been surprised to see the big constable reporting for duty that morning. He was pale and had lost a lot of weight, but he seemed keen enough and despite the crutches, he moved about as fast as most of his able bodied colleagues. In spite of the initial antagonism that had existed between them, Hilary had to admit to herself that she was pleased to have his solidly reassuring bulk back in harness. She had missed his support.

"If you like, Jeff, you can accompany me in the area car, rather than be stuck in an office. It isn't strictly light duties, but it should be far more interesting and I won't let you get involved in anything strenuous."

Maddox nodded across the briefing room at the sergeant and she went back to her allocation of duties. He had not been particularly keen to return to work so soon, but a visitation in the early hours of the morning had rather forced him to do so.

He had come slowly out of a deep sleep and his eyes had jerked open as he spotted the shadowy figure at the end of his bed.

"McConnel, what the fuck are you doing here, Man?"

The bearded hippy put a finger to his lips and the policeman narrowed his eyes.

"What do you want? I am still on the sick – know what I mean?"

"I want to talk to you, Maddox. You owe me one remember. I gather that you are very much on the mend and we have a lot to sort out between us. My bruises still ache when the weather is cold."

Maddox said nothing. He had been told about the work McConnel had done on his leg and knew that he probably owed his life to the bearded man. The thought made him flush with shame for his own actions where McConnel was concerned, but it was too late to turn the clock back. Now it seemed that the hippy had come for his revenge.

"How the fuck did you get in, McConnel? I locked everything before coming to bed."

McConnel merely grinned and sat down on the end of the bed.

"It wasn't difficult, but that isn't the point. I want to talk to you about your sergeant."

"Sergeant Bedwell?"

Green eyes gleamed above the tangled hair of McConnel's face.

"The very one, Maddox. Hilary means a lot to me and she needs someone to watch her back. She is in an invidious position at the moment and I can't help her. You can though."

Sitting up in bed, Maddox swung his legs over the side and frowned down at his bandages.

"Don't be daft, Man. She doesn't need help from me. Hilary Bedwell is a tough nut and a damned good copper. She also has a great future in front of her which you are doing your best to fuck up, McConnel."

The bearded man nodded and there was a sombre look in his eye.

"I know that Maddox – by God I know that and it worries me, but there seems little that she or I can do about the situation right now."

"Just back off, Man. Stay away from her and let her get on with her career."

Standing up from the bed, McConnel walked to a window and looked sightlessly out into a somewhat unkempt garden.

"You need a gardener, Maddox," he said absently. "There are more weeds than grass in your lawn."

He swung around to face the police officer once more.

"Listen to me, Maddox. Hilary Bedwell is a damned fine copper as you say and a lovely person to boot, but she needs looking after and you are the only one who can do that. You know damned well how a pretty young woman can be shunted about and left out to dry in the police force. Her future depends on good results and you can ensure that she gets those. She is going to have a rough time over the next few months and I want you to take her under your wing."

"Hold on a minute McConnel." Maddox held up a big hand. "What would you know about a woman's lot in the police force? What makes you think I can do anything to ensure Hilary Bedwell's well being? I'm not bloody superman you know and besides, my leg is fucked – know what I mean?"

"No it isn't, Maddox. I've been keeping tabs on you and I know that you are about ready to go back to work. Come on Man – with your experience, you can sort Hilary's problems out for her. You can be a mentor of sorts and make sure she doesn't drop herself into any further trouble."

Although he spoke quietly, there was considerable intensity in his voice and his eyes held the big policeman like a pin holding a dead butterfly to a card. For his part, Maddox wasn't sure what McConnel was getting at, but he felt as though he was a clay statue being moulded into shape by an experienced sculptor. His limbs were suddenly weak and he knew that he would do exactly as his visitor wanted.

"Where are you going to be?"

McConnel shrugged.

"Here and there I suppose. I will keep an eye on her too, but you are the only one in a position to really help."

Maddox frowned.

"Listen McConnel, you realise that our Hilary has a huge crush on you, don't you? Why such a pretty girl should fancy a toe rag like you I just cannot imagine, but she does – know what I mean?"

McConnel nodded matter of factly and his eyes twinkled. Something lurked behind the mockery though and Maddox was aware of it, but couldn't identify the emotion.

"Yes I know, Maddox and I feel much the same about her, but there is nothing that either of us can do about it, so feelings just have to be forgotten.

'I reckon you are pretty keen on the lass yourself, Maddox, so just make sure you give her as much support as you can. You owe me more than you know, but this you can do for Hilary herself."

Maddox looked suddenly truculent at being ordered about by the bearded man, but there was a steely look in the green eyes that quickly subdued him.

"You are a hard man, Jeff Maddox." McConnel went on quietly. "But believe me, I am a bloody sight harder, so don't let me down. You are also a bloody good plod, for all your hot-headed ways. You are in the best position to ensure that our girl gets on in her chosen career and I will be keeping an eye on you to make sure you do just that."

He paused and the only sound in the room was the heavy breathing of the two men. After a while, McConnel went on.

"You might not like that idea, Maddox, but there is sod all you can do about it. Even without the bad leg, I am far too strong for you and while you might think you have the law on your side, the next time you come after me you will need more than that silly little stick, you carry around. It makes a better splint than a cosh anyway."

Maddox looked discomfited again and after a long moment of silent eye contact, he held out a brawny hand.

"Yeah, well; sorry about that, McConnel. I let myself get a bit carried away that night. Mind you, it wasn't all my fault. You were bloody asking for trouble in that place – know what I mean? What the hell were you doing there anyway?"

The words sounded defensive and McConnel grinned as he rubbed his jaw line, ignoring the proffered hand.

"I'll say you got carried away, Jeff Maddox. As I told you, the bruises still hurt and that was bloody weeks ago. Anyway, it is all forgotten as far as I am concerned and I have arranged one last little gift for the lovely sergeant before I drop out of her life. After that, you and she are on your own. Just make sure she has your support in everything."

"What sort of gift?"

"You'll see Man. Report back for duty today and I'll guarantee you a really nice surprise."

This time he did shake Maddox' hand and the two men exchanged another long look of silent communion. Moments later, McConnel was gone.

Maddox dragged his mind back to the present and tried to forget the strange visitation. It was obvious that McConnel had his own agenda, but for the life of him, the big constable could not figure out what that might be. His thoughts were interrupted when Hilary was hailed from the door by a reception clerk.

"What is it, Mike?"

She sounded irritable and Maddox knew that McConnel's apparent disappearance was still weighing heavily on her mind.

"There's a punter to see you at the front desk, Sarge."

For a moment, hope flared in her eyes, but it faded as the young man went on.

"Well dressed, spivvy type who will only speak with you and won't tell me what it is all about. Sorry Sarge, I did try to find out what he wants."

Maddox frowned at her obvious disappointment, then hauled himself out of the chair and tried to find a comfortable position on the crutches. He didn't really need them to walk about, but they gave him a ready made advantage if there was any serious work to be avoided. Hilary smiled at him as she bustled out of the door.

"Be with you in a moment, Jeff. I'll just see what this chap wants. Wait for me by the area car will you. I have a feeling in my water that today is the day Thursday Joe makes his first mistake."

"Huh!"

PC Maddox was obviously unconvinced, but he duly made his way out to the station car park and let himself into the passenger seat of the area car.

CHAPTER ELEVEN

The little man was obviously nervous. At first glance, he was smartly attired in a hideously loud check jacket with what appeared to be some sort of regimental tie, but his brown trousers were baggy and wrinkled, while his collar appeared frayed and grimy. His hair was uncombed and starting to go grey and he sat stiffly on a bench in the waiting room. Hilary studied him through the one-way glass before going through to see what he wanted. Despite his jacket and the tie, he was unshaven and hollow-eyed, yet there was something vaguely familiar about the man that she couldn't quite put her finger on.

"Who is he, Mike?" She asked the reception clerk on the way through and the young man shrugged.

"No idea, Sarge. He wouldn't tell me his name and insists on speaking to you and nobody else. I told him you were busy, but he said he would wait as long as it takes. Just wouldn't take no for an answer I'm afraid."

Hilary frowned.

"He looks familiar somehow, but I can't put a name to him. Damn, I should have asked Jeff Maddox to come through. He would have known who the bloke is."

"Shall I get him for you, Sarge?"

After a brief hesitation, she shook her head.

"No, I sent him out to the car and don't want to put him through the walk back here. From the look of him, I don't really think he should be back at work anyway.

'Oh well, the only way to find out who this chappie is, is to go and ask him I suppose."

Pulling the heavy glass windows aside, Hilary leaned over the reception counter and called to the little man.

"Hello Sir: I am Sergeant Bedwell. I understand you wanted to see me?"

A look of relieved apprehension spread across the man's face and as he stood up, Hilary had a feeling of sudden recognition coupled with a sense of shock. She shook her head as though to clear it. Surely she had to be wrong? Once again, she wished she had Jeff Maddox with her. This surely couldn't be happening.

The little man shambled over to the counter and although she knew that her initial instinct was right, Hilary couldn't help reflecting that there was something very different about him. The arrogant little fighting cock she remembered, arguing with the custody sergeant had been completely transformed into this pathetically humble creature. His shoulders were bowed and all the fight and bluster had gone out of him, leaving a mere reflection of the Razor Wallace she remembered.

"I believe you have been looking for me," he told her and his voice was so soft that she strained to hear him. "I am Harold Wallace. People call me Razor and I think I need to talk to you."

For a moment, Hilary could not think what to say. The entire force – and every other police force in the country – had indeed been searching for this man over the previous three and a half weeks. His photograph and description had been circulated to every officer in the land as well as all ports, airports and other points of possible exit from the country. He had been classified as extremely dangerous and the advice had been that if seen, he was to be approached with extreme caution.

Yet here he stood in front of her – meek, humble and a long way from being dangerous. If this was Razor Wallace it was hardly surprising he hadn't been found. He looked like any other little man struggling to make ends meet in the city. This surely could not be the violent criminal who had so callously gunned down Jeff Maddox.

It was the man himself who settled the matter. He must have sensed her doubt and placed a supermarket bag that was obviously heavy on the counter in front of her.

"This might help," he whispered and watched as she tore open the loose package with hesitant fingers. As she drew the wrapping aside, a large, black revolver fell on to the counter between them.

Hardly believing what she was seeing, Hilary glanced at the gun, then at Razor Wallace. He might not look the part of a hardened villain, but the weapon was unmistakably lethal and suddenly she felt her blood run cold.

***

"That was a turn up for the books hey, Sarge? Not in a thousand years would I have expected Razor Wallace to turn himself in. The man is a scrote of the first order, but I've never thought of him as anything other than a hard bastard – know what I mean? This is one scumbag who I would not have thought would lose his bottle, whatever the circumstances. Not in a million years I wouldn't – know what I mean? Wonder where the hard arsed little sod has been hiding?"

"I would have expected him in sunny Spain or the French Riviera." Hilary smiled with evident satisfaction. Razor Wallace turning himself in had proved an excellent start to her day. "I nearly wet my pants when I realised who he was. I wonder what made him come in, Jeff. Do you reckon he ran out of food or something? It seems doubtful. I know they didn't get a lot from the building society job, but it must have been enough to keep them going for a while?"

"Perhaps someone got at him." Maddox sounded thoughtful as an awful suspicion gnawed at his senses. "You know how the villains get twitchy when a copper is shot? Perhaps a few of the big boys paid him a visit."

Yet in his heart, the big constable knew full well who had persuaded Wallace to give himself up. He didn't know how it had been done, but the evidence was surely there. What were the words McConnel had used?

"I have arranged one last little gift for the lovely sergeant," and "report back for duty today and I'll guarantee you a nice surprise."

The gift and the surprise were obviously wrapped up in the person of Razor Wallace who at that very moment would be pouring his heart out to the Suits in the CID offices. Whistling in considerable astonishment to himself, Maddox wondered what pressures the hippy had exerted on an experienced villain like Wallace to make him turn himself in.

He was about to talk it out with the sergeant when the vehicle radio blared into life.

"Sergeant Bedwell: Control – do you read over?"

"Answer it please, Jeff." Hilary jerked her chin at the handset and concentrated on steering them through the traffic. "It might be something important to brighten my day even further."

"Go ahead Control; she is listening."

"Ten Three please Sergeant; the Chief Inspector wants to see you."

"Okay, on our way."

"I wonder what he wants now?" Hilary mused and Maddox laughed aloud.

"Probably about to grant you instant promotion for bringing in Razor Wallace, Skip."

"I didn't bring him in Jeff. He came in. I've no idea why he should have asked for me personally. Okay, I am dealing with the case where he was distributing gear with those two youngsters, but other than that, he doesn't know me from a bar of soap."

"You don't have to tell the Guv'nor that, Sarge. Let him think you have a hot line to the underworld and you will be a Chief Super in no time."

Hilary giggled at the thought and turned the car into the station yard.

"Wait for me please, Jeff. I'm sure this won't take long."

With that she was gone – a trim, pretty figure, very much in control of her own destiny in a fiercely male preserve. Maddox watched her go with a rare smile showing on his craggy features.

***

Having knocked briskly on the office door, Hilary moved cautiously inside at the grunted command from within.

Chief Inspector Bolton looked up momentarily from his paperwork and a little to Hilary's surprise, his gaze was distinctly antagonistic. His eyes were cold and the angles of his face were set in uncompromising lines. Despite a 'no smoking' sign prominently displayed on one wall, blue smoke billowed from his pipe and drifted through the office like an evil-smelling cloud. Hilary caught her breath and struggled to hold back a coughing fit. A non smoker herself, she had grown accustomed to the fact that most of her colleagues seemed addicted to nicotine despite the many 'no smoking' signs scattered around the police station. However, Bolton used a particularly vile brand of tobacco and the resulting fumes were acrid and harsh on the throat.

"You sent for me, Sir?"

"Indeed I did, Sergeant. Indeed I did."

His tone was cold and Hilary wondered what she had done wrong this time. It could not have anything to do with McConnel, as she had not seen him for weeks. Besides, she ought to have been very much in favour after the unexpected success of the early afternoon. What on earth was bugging the

Guv'nor now? Standing uncomfortably to attention in front of the desk, she waited anxiously while Bolton went on with his paperwork.

At last he seemed to have finished. Carefully placing his pen exactly in the centre of the desk, the Officer in Charge looked up at Hilary, almost as though he had never seen her before. She shifted uneasily at the hostility in his gaze and suddenly found that her heart was hammering inside her chest. Could this possibly be a joke? But no, Don Bolton had the reputation for being a stickler for the rules and he was unlikely to lower himself to the level of practical tomfoolery that so many of his subordinates seemed to enjoy. He was not that sort of man.

After gazing at his sergeant with unconcealed annoyance for almost a minute, Bolton silently gestured at the office chair and Hilary sat down gratefully, careful to keep knees together, her back straight and an expression of respectful attention on her face.

"Yes I did send for you, Sergeant Bedwell. Firstly I want to know why Razor Wallace should have asked for you when he came in earlier?"

"I have absolutely no idea, Sir. I was as surprised as anyone else."

"It doesn't make sense, Sergeant. Wallace and our local Suits have known each other for years, yet when he hands himself in, he asks for a uniformed officer who hasn't been at this nick for five minutes. And a girl still wet behind the ears at that. It seems difficult to believe and I can't help wondering about your contacts in the criminal world."

"I have no contacts in the criminal world, Sir." Hilary exploded indignantly. "I was every bit as surprised as anyone else that he asked for me, but there was nothing sinister about it, I can assure you."

"What do you know about Thursday Joe?"

The abrupt change of subject took Hilary by surprise. She had been prepared to defend herself on the subject of Razor Wallace but the barked question on such a different tack left her completely at a loss for words. She wondered whether it might be some sort of a test to see whether she had her finger on the pulse of all the matters on hand. If so, it was not going to get the Chief Inspector very far. Sergeant Hilary Bedwell had made herself into an expert on the subject of Thursday Joe. Yet something still niggled at her mind.

"You have asked me this before, Sir and I told you what I knew then."

"Humour me, Sergeant. Tell me again. There is plenty of time."

"Okay;" she hesitated as she tried to get her thoughts together; "now that Razor Wallace is banged up, Thursday Joe has to be the most troublesome and annoying villain on our books. He has been responsible for nearly a hundred housebreakings and burglaries over the past year or so and I am sure there are many more that haven't been reported.

'He concentrates on country cottages, only takes cash and does a minimum of damage. He is obviously an expert with all types of locks and alarm systems and so far, nobody has even caught sight of him. Nine times out of ten, the victims don't realise they have been done over until they miss their money.

'He only operates – as far as we know – on Thursday afternoons, which accounts for the nickname and in spite of numerous extra patrols and plain clothes surveillance teams operating on those days, he has remained at large and apparently without effort.

'In one of his earlier jobs..." she paused for breath... "in one of his earlier jobs, a fragmentary fingerprint was found, but we haven't been able to match it up with any known villain. As far as DNA is concerned, he must wear gloves and covering clothing, as not a trace has ever been found."

She stammered to a halt and the Chief Inspector grunted, although Hilary wasn't sure whether the sound denoted approval or otherwise. Throughout her recital, his eyes had not left her face and they still held a look of deep malevolence that she could not understand.

Although Don Bolton was a gruff, bellicose character, she knew that he was a softie at heart and had always held her in high esteem. He had told her so himself on a number of occasions and she always had the feeling that he was keeping a personal eye on her progress. Why then was he so angry with her? It didn't make sense, but Hilary knew that she had to be patient and wait to see what developed.

"There isn't much more to tell, Sir," she went on slowly. "As I said, Thursday Joe prefers the more isolated dwellings, but he targeted Ashville housing estate a few weeks ago and even though we flooded the area with plain clothes officers, he still managed to do seven houses the following Thursday as well. In each case, he nicked considerable sums of money, which were apparently lying around. The owners reckoned so anyway. It doesn't seem likely on an estate like that, but we have no choice but to take their word for the losses."

"You have done your homework, Sergeant," Bolton admitted grudgingly. "When did you last see your tame crusty?"

Once again Hilary was confused. There seemed no rhyme or reason for the sudden change of subject and she couldn't help wondering what had upset her superior officer so much.

"Not since the day of the building society job, Sir. He might possibly have moved on, as nobody seems to have seen him of late, even though I have put him up for a reward.

'As you know, Sir." She added hastily.

"Yes I do know, Sergeant. I recommended it too, blithering nincompoop that I am!"

Frowning heavily, he concentrated on easing a blockage from his pipe and Hilary waited in silence for him to speak again.

'Ah yes, Sergeant Bedwell, I well remember the day PC Maddox was shot. Wasn't that when I stumbled across a tender little scene in the High Street between you and your Mr McConnel? I don't know what you were discussing with the bloke, Sergeant, but it looked a very cosy moment to me."

Hilary felt herself flushing once again and struggled to control the anger boiling in her chest. She had no idea what she had done to upset her irascible superior, but she did not see why she should be the butt of his tirade. Nor could she see what relevance her relationship – such as it was – with McConnel had to either the bank robbery or the misdeeds of Thursday Joe.

"It was not, Sir," she began hotly. "We were just…" She paused and then broke off defiantly. "Besides, I think that is my business and I do not see what my personal life has to do with anything…."

"You will, Sergeant; you will."

Having uttered that grim little promise, Chief Inspector Bolton turned back to the papers on his desk. He leafed purposefully through them while Hilary subsided in her chair, wishing desperately that she knew what was going on.

Ever since McConnel had disappeared after performing miracles on Jeff Maddox' leg, Hilary had made a determined effort to get the charismatic hippy out of her mind. It had not been simple to do and she found herself wondering about him at the most inopportune moments, but she had felt she was making some progress. She was pragmatic enough to know and accept that his developing influence on her emotions could only lead to disaster.

Her career had to come first and the police system did not allow for such as McConnel. She did not want her feelings for the man to wreck her life as a copper and had made a conscious decision to stay away from Swanwick Beacon. Work offered the only palliative and for three weeks, Hilary had submerged her burgeoning affection for McConnel in the routine of her daily duties.

It had not been an easy decision for Hilary to make, but once it was made, she felt a sense of considerable relief. Now it seemed that she was not going to be allowed to get away from her feelings quite so easily. Chief Inspector Bolton obviously had his own thoughts on the matter and seemed determined not to let it drop. Anger surged in Hilary's bosom once again and she scowled at the top of Bolton's head.

Almost as though he felt the gesture, the big man looked up, leaned back in his chair and stared moodily at her.

"We have had a development in the Thursday Joe case, Sergeant," he told her slowly, his eyes never leaving her face. "He has been seen and actually spoken to by a witness, although the man obviously didn't realise it at the time."

Hilary forgot her sullen resentment of the senior officer in excitement at the news.

"That is good news, Sir. With a good description, we will at least know what we are looking for. May I have a look?"

She held out her hand and Bolton wordlessly passed a single sheet of paper across the desk. Hilary read eagerly.

The witness statement had been taken by a CID sergeant and briefly outlined the facts as they related to the witness. It seemed that the previous Thursday, a householder, Mr Joseph Seward Wemyss of 91 Warburton Close, Ashville Estate had returned home in mid afternoon and seen a scruffily dressed man leaving the house next door. They had exchanged greetings and the scruffy one had even paused for a brief chat. It was only when the owner of number 93 returned home later in the day that discovery of the break in had taken place and Mr Wemyss recalled the afternoon encounter.

"I didn't want to report it at first," he had told the DS. "He seemed such a nice young man that I just didn't believe he could have been a criminal."

"They always do," Hilary muttered to herself. "Criminals don't go around in black eye masks and arrowed pyjamas with bags marked 'swag' on their shoulders any more. They are usually quite indistinguishable from their fellow citizens and many of them seem to be very nice people."

Looking up, she intercepted a sardonic look from Don Bolton, but the Chief Inspector waved her on.

She skipped over the next few paragraphs and turned to the detailed description of the suspect that was given at the end of the statement. The typed words, stark on their clean white background seemed to burn deep holes in her brain.

'White male; approximately thirty years of age: six foot, with long dark hair and full, tangled beard. Dressed in brown pullover and maroon trousers with coloured beads hanging around his neck. Clothing described as 'old, torn and in very dirty condition.' Also wore heavy, gardening boots and green woollen headgear of the type known as a 'bobble hat.' Colour of eyes believed to be green or hazel, but when suspect spoke, his voice was described as being 'deep and soft, with no trace of an accent.'

As she lowered the typewritten form, Hilary absently noticed that her hand was shaking. The baldly worded description left her feeling nauseous and on the point of tears. In spite of herself, she read it again.

'White male' – well that described fifty odd percent of the population. 'Approximately thirty years of age' – that certainly fitted. 'Six foot' – that was roughly his height. 'Long, dark hair and full, tangled beard' – that could only be one person in this locality. Her lips curled in shameful embarrassment. The clothing described was also apt, although the description might have fitted almost any male - and most of the female – members of the travelling fraternity. It was the hat that decided it for Hilary. That green bobble hat was McConnel's trademark and she remembered wondering whether he wore it to bed at night. He had even been wearing the damned thing in the ambulance after his beating.

The description of the suspect's voice was the final clincher. Reading the words again, Hilary could almost hear McConnel speaking. 'Deep and soft, with no trace of an accent' – what a terribly fitting description of McConnel's quiet baritone.

The Chief Inspector was still gazing at her and the sardonic gleam in his eye seemed even more pronounced.

"Any comment, Sergeant Bedwell?"

Hilary frowned at her Boss but she didn't see him. Her face was flushed a deep brick-red, her mind was on McConnel and her feelings were both confused and bitter.

There surely couldn't be any doubt. She looked at the statement again, but the words hadn't changed. McConnel was Thursday Joe and she had been in danger of falling in love with the man. Hilary's eyes narrowed in anger and her lips straightened into a thin, hard line. He was not going to get away with it. He had made an utter fool of her and nobody did that to Hilary Bedwell.

Still holding the sheet of paper in one trembling hand, Hilary rose to her feet and stood looking down on the Chief Inspector. He waved her irritably back into her seat.

"Do sit down and stop being so bloody melodramatic, Sergeant Bedwell." He growled, although his tone had softened slightly. "You understand now why I called you in?"

Hilary nodded wordlessly, not trusting herself to speak. Her stomach felt cramped and sore, while a headache was building behind her eyes. A feeling of irretrievable loss permeated her system, but it was overlaid by a sense of betrayal. A spark of anger threatened to explode from deep within her stomach and her knees felt weak with reaction.

Hesitantly, she sank back into the chair. She had been an unutterable fool and she knew it. She had risked everything for McConnel and he had been laughing at her all the time.

"What a bloody idiot he must have thought I was." She muttered and Bolton wasn't sure whether she was addressing him or herself.

The Chief Inspector nodded grimly.

"You were a damned fool, Sergeant. That much is not in doubt. You are a good copper and might yet go far, but on this occasion you let your hormones do all the thinking. The question is, what are we going to do about it?"

Hilary looked across the desk at the big man and all the life seemed to have drained from her face. She had gone very pale and her features seemed to have melted together, the gentle powdering of freckles across her nose suddenly appearing like a slash of war paint in the office lights. Reading the bald facts of the witness statement seemed to have reduced a lively, good looking young police sergeant into an old woman in the space of a few seconds.

Chief Inspector Bolton was horrified by the sudden change and hid his feelings by relighting his pipe. When it was drawing to his satisfaction and the entire office was wreathed in clouds of dense blue smoke, he spoke to Hilary again and this time, his tone had noticeably softened.

"Do you feel up to taking on this case yourself, Hilary?"

She nodded vigorously and there was a sudden gleam of moisture in her eyes.

"Oh yes please, Sir. I'll have the bastard picked up straight away and handle the interrogation myself. His blandishments certainly won't be working on me any more."

Bolton smiled tightly and held up one big hand.

"Not so fast, Sergeant Bedwell. I am taking one hell of a chance by letting you anywhere near this one, you realise that? I shouldn't allow you within miles of Thursday Joe or McConnel or whatever you call him. You are far too closely involved. The ACC. will have my knackers for a door knocker if this goes wrong.

'On the other hand, I think you have been well and truly taken for a ride by this toe rag and I want to see you bring him in. No rushing in balls and all though. This one has to be done softly and by the book. He might look like an arsehole, but McConnel is obviously pretty switched on to have run us ragged for so long. He also speaks too much like a toff for us to take any chances with him. I reckon there is more to the man than meets the eye somehow and that could make things difficult for us.

'Still, I don't suppose you will make the same mistake again, will you?"

Hilary shook her head miserably and the Chief Inspector went on.

"For the moment, I've called for an identifit artist from Headquarters to see if we can get a recognisable likeness out of the fellow Wemyss. I want you to do a full check on McConnel's antecedents before you go charging in. For all we know, he might have form as long as his arm. The more we can find out about the man before we pick him up, the easier it will be to nail him."

"For all you know, I might be a big time villain on the run, Sergeant Hilary."

How well she remembered him saying those very words while they were drinking coffee. She remembered the gentle mockery of his smile and the compelling power of his gaze. How he must have been laughing inwardly at her naiveté.

Shaking her head at the ambivalence of her thoughts, Hilary felt an unexpected surge of affection for her irascible Superior. Many senior officers would have relished her mistake and taken full advantage, but Bolton was giving her another chance and putting his own head on the block in the process.

"I won't let you down, Sir. I promise you. I'll handle the whole scene myself and give it priority."

"Ask Jeff Maddox to give you a hand, Girl. He is very experienced at this sort of thing and will keep you on the right track. I would suggest you start off with a PNC check on McConnel. Even though the partial dab we found hasn't yet been matched, the computer might hold something on the bloke."

Hilary stood up again and there was indecision on her face.

"I'll have to find out more about him first, Sir. I don't even know his Christian names. He did mention them once, but now I have no idea whether he was telling the truth or trying to put me off the scent."

"What?" The Chief Inspector looked incredulous. "Are you telling me that you can have it off with the bloke and not even know who he is?"

"I was NOT 'having it off' with him, Sir." She banged a small fist down on the desk in frustration. "He was friendly and gave me some good information and that is all there was to it."

Bolton made no effort to disguise his scepticism and Hilary felt herself flush again with embarrassed anger. There had been more to her relationship with McConnel than that and both she and Don Bolton knew it.

"Okay Sergeant," the big man rumbled. "I won't press the point, but we'd better get a thorough check done on him as soon as we can."

"Yes Sir."

Hilary turned to leave the office, the case file bulky under her arm. As she reached the door, the officer in charge of the station called out again.

"Sergeant Bedwell."

She turned slowly, knowing what was coming.

"Yes Sir?"

For a long moment, Don Bolton held her gaze and when he spoke, his voice was very hard.

"Don't balls this one up, Hilary. Make sure you have PC Maddox along when you nick the bloke and let him do the talking. I am taking one hell of a chance with you, My Girl and my career is as much on the line as yours if this case does a bubble. Keep your hormones in check and don't let me down please."

Hilary nodded grimly and left the room without bothering to reply. Walking down the corridor towards her office, her mind churned with possibilities and the chance to get her own back on the man who had betrayed her so badly. Sticking her head into the Control Room, she snapped at a radio operator.

"Find Jeff Maddox for me please. I left him half asleep in the area car, but I want him in my office right now."

"Roger Sarge."

The operator bent to his set, but Hilary didn't stay to hear what was said. Leaving the Control Room, she hurried to her office where she examined herself critically in a mirror behind the door. Her face was still pale and there was a sullen tilt to her mouth that only added to her anger and self disgust.

"How could you be such a damned fool, Hilary Bedwell?" She asked her reflection, but the blue eyes that stared back at her held only sadness.

There was no logical answer to the question.

CHAPTER TWELVE

He sat motionless in the shadow of an old Oak tree. Above him, light faded from the great dome of the sky and darkness slowly descended to envelop the world. The evening star winked angrily down on him but McConnel was only vaguely aware of the subtle change in his surroundings.

Absorbed with his own problems, the bearded man had come once again to his favourite spot in the woods for some tranquil meditation, but his mind was confused and a jumble of contradictory thoughts and emotions struggled for precedence in his tormented brain. He had always been a man of decision and a man with strong principles, yet the principles seemed to have deserted him and he just did not know what to do.

His problems centred on the person of Hilary Bedwell and he could not get her out of his mind. He thought about her all the time; worried about her, wondered what she was doing and ached to be with her. He wanted to see her face, touch her hand and enjoy her tinkling laugh. He wanted to put his arms around her and hold her to him, yet he knew that it could not be and the knowledge was torturing him.

Desperately trying to clear his brain, he made a determined effort to meditate. Breathing deeply, he leaned back against the tree and concentrated on the colour yellow. Allowing his mind to fill to its limit with the colour, he let it overflow and spread slowly through his system, filling his pores and oozing into the extremities of his body. The feeling of colour seemed to move up with his bloodstream until it once again filtered through the cells of his brain before gradually disappearing from his consciousness. Clearing his mind again, he paused to breathe and relax his muscles then went through the process again, this time with the colour orange. Orange was followed by red in the meditational sequence, but as the red moved up through his legs and lower torso, it seemed to take a great leap and exploded in his brain with fiery lances of blood. His veins sizzled in sudden torment and a violent shudder racked his body. Shaking his head in anguished desperation,

McConnel brought himself back to the present and his own personal problems.

Always honest with himself, McConnel knew that he was in love. There was no rhyme or reason to the feeling, but it was there in his soul and there was nothing he could do to alter that. He had thought himself immune to such idiocies, but he could no longer hide from the reality. He loved Hilary Bedwell and that was all there was to it. She loved him too, even if she wouldn't admit it to herself. It was apparent in the way she looked at him, the way she spoke to him and the spark in her eyes when they were together. Yet it was a love that for both of them could never be admitted. His entire life had become an agony of frustrated indecision and there seemed little he could do to change that. He wanted to share his existence with Hilary, but their paths through life were far too different for there to be any chance of compromise. Although neither of them were married and were technically free to spend their lives together, it wasn't like that in reality. They both had ties too large to allow that happy eventuality. Hilary Bedwell was wedded to the police service and he was wedded to Ellie and his life as a shiftless drifter, as surely as though banns had been read and the necessary nuptial service been performed. There was no way out of their ties for either of them.

As a shiftless drop out from the orderly world of society, he might just have got away with cleaning himself up and changing his way of life. He might even have been able to settle down to a regular job and having somehow transformed himself into a respected member of the community, been able to convince Hilary Bedwell of his love for her. In ideal circumstances, they would have found so much common ground between them – a neutral plane where their affections could mingle and develop in harmony. It was a wonderful dream and McConnel smiled to himself.

But it was only a dream. He pulled himself back to reality. This was the real world and he had to abide by its rules. Hilary Bedwell was a police officer, dedicated to her job and with a promising career opening up in front of her. Her prospects were infinite and if he pursued the relationship, his own past was sure to come out and do irreparable damage to those prospects. As a man who had done unspeakable things in unspeakable circumstances, he could never settle to orderly life and his presence in Hilary's existence might well wreck her chances of further promotion and eventually tear their relationship apart, leaving each of them badly hurt and even more alone than they had been before.

McConnel was no stranger to the Service mind and he could imagine the sacrifices that would be necessary on Hilary's part if they were to have any chance at all of being together on a permanent basis. It was altogether too much to ask of anyone, even if she did share his deep feelings and he only had his own instinct to say that she did. Much as McConnel had always trusted his instincts, his self confidence was low and he wondered in his heart whether he was right about Hilary's love for him. He had sensed her confusion from the start and while it had been amusing at first, it had rapidly developed into an added factor in his own misery.

With an anguished moan, McConnel looked down at his hands. Even in the darkness, he could sense how filthy they were and he was suddenly filled with self-disgust. This surely was not how he was meant to spend his days. There had to be more to life that the utter squalor in which he existed. His activities in the past had often sickened him and left him with a deep sense of self-loathing, but at least he had been good at them and could take a certain pride in his own competence. He had done everything required of him with cold-blooded ferocity and a blankness in his mind that cushioned shock and regrets. In his own horrific little world, he had at least been Somebody.

Now he was a nothing – in police parlance, a low life or oxygen thief. He was no use to man or beast, just a filthy, useless escapee from the real world. Even his body had deteriorated. The lean, hard-muscled frame, he had been so proud of had softened and filled out. He carried a definite bulge at his waist and even though he was fit for his age, he found himself gasping for breath whenever he was forced to run even a short distance.

Feeling a sense of infinite sadness, McConnel automatically corrected himself. He was of use, even if it was only to Ellie and the brats. They needed him and it was his responsibility to look after them. He should be devoting his life to their welfare, not mooning about over a woman who was completely unattainable whatever might happen. He smiled tightly as he wondered what Ellie's reaction would be if she ever learned who he really was. How would she take the fripperies of the life he had left behind him. How would she react to the power and privilege he had abandoned and could so easily take up again.

Raising his face to the spangled heavens, McConnel laughed aloud, but the sound was filled with despair. He had dropped out of that life because he couldn't take the double standards and hypocrisy involved. He had joined the crumpled fraternity of Society's rejects to escape the horrors of the world in which he had so excelled. What else was there in life for him now? Even if he could somehow persuade Hilary Bedwell to live with him, how would they survive? And could he really abandon Ellie? She was not equipped to cope with life in the real world and besides, he owed her a great deal.

It was Ellie who had nursed him through the nightmares. Ellie who had held his sweaty head to her bosom when he thrashed and cried out in terrified remembrance. She had never questioned him or pried into his antecedents and the reasons for his torment. Even now when she was worried and upset with him, she still loved him with a faithful subservience that was frightening in its intensity. She had also borne him two children and if there was perhaps some doubt about Lisa's parentage, the baby was definitely his own and something to be proud of. Not an incidental to be abandoned for an unattainable dream.

In his bitter confusion, McConnel felt tears roll hotly through the tangled hair around his face. His ribs ached with the intensity of his emotions and he felt a great, desolate emptiness in his heart. Desperately he searched his inner being for the colours that offered him lonely solace. Red, orange, yellow, green, blue, indigo and violet – each one associated with a different chakra or wheel of the body. He would finish the routine with black and in spite of its normally dark connotations, it somehow balanced out the meditational sequence. He always envisioned the colours in the same order and each colour had its own deeply spiritual significance. McConnel let them waft gently through his being in turn and slowly – ever so slowly – peace returned to his soul.

As the night sky paled to the East and the sun glowed orange beneath the horizon, he rose slowly to his feet and began to walk.

***

Hilary searched through her memory while Jeff Maddox watched her carefully. The big constable was slumped in a chair in the sergeant's office with the witness statement of the man Wemyss in one hand and she was trying to remember the first names that McConnel had mentioned to her.

"Why not just try McConnel, Sarge? If this silly bugger, Wemyss is right, McConnel is bound to have form and perhaps he is registered under the one name – know what I mean?"

"That isn't really likely Jeff, is it? You know what sticklers for detail CRO are. Anyway, I thought you didn't believe Wemyss' statement."

"No, I bloody well don't!" Maddox frowned as he lit a cigarette and looked for somewhere to throw the match. Hilary's desk was devoid of ashtrays and he eventually threw it down on the floor behind him. "The description fits McConnel like a glove, but there is something not quite right about it – know what I mean? Perhaps it is too bloody accurate. I don't know what it is, but I don't like it."

"You must admit that McConnel is not a difficult chap to describe, Jeff. His appearance has to be pretty unique and that damned bobble hat is unmistakable."

"Yeah, I know that, Skip, but I don't care what else he might be, I would not put McConnel down as a regular villain – know what I mean? For all the life he leads and the fucking horrible way he looks, he is straight up at heart."

Hilary looked momentarily amused.

"Changed your tune a bit, haven't you, Jeff? I seem to recall you using the words 'scrote' and 'scumbag' fairly regularly to describe McConnel. What happened to all that?"

The big fellow grinned.

"Yeah, well, maybe I had the bugger wrong at first, Sarge – know what I mean? We have talked since then and there is something about the bloke that is pretty damned straight. I'd put money on the fact that he is not Thursday Joe, no matter what this bloke Wemyss has to say. Perhaps he did see McConnel, but I'll bet your man was not breaking into anything at the time."

"He is not 'my man,' PC Maddox," Hilary said primly, but there was little conviction in her voice. "I cannot see how he can get out of this one though. No matter what you say, that description is pretty exact."

Maddox opened his mouth to say more, but she suddenly held up one hand to stop him.

"Hold on a moment, Jeff. It is coming to me. Yes.. yes… I've got it. Alexander Herbert, those were the names he gave me."

She remembered the bearded man's shy smile when he told her about the names and for a moment, she felt a deep stab of pain in her heart. Standing up abruptly, she took the statement out of Maddox' hand.

"Come on, let's go, Jeff. Time to check McConnel out on the PNC. You can hit the keys for me and let's see what we can find."

Four minutes later, Jeff Maddox was ensconced in a chair in front of a computer screen in the control room. Hilary pulled up another chair and sat at his shoulder, while the radio operators looked at them in some surprise. Requests for information on the Police National Computer were normally routed through one of them, but the pretty sergeant and her big colleague were obviously on a mission of their own.

"What's your PNC password, Skipper?"

Hilary gave it to him and he typed it in, using two spatulate middle fingers to hit the keys.

"Okay, let's see what it gives us. Vehicle or person?" He clicked on the 'person' box and a computerised form sprang up on the screen.

"Known criminal - no. Male or female – male; ethnic grouping – caucasian. Full names? You sure about those two, Sarge?"

Hilary nodded briskly. She could still hear McConnel telling her and see his smile in her mind. Shaking the memories away, she concentrated on the big officer beside her.

"Sure Jeff. Alexander and Herbert were the names he gave me."

"Okay;" Maddox entered McConnel in the relevant box and Alexander Herbert in the spaces reserved for 'forenames – if known.'

"Date of birth?" He raised heavy eyebrows at the sergeant and Hilary frowned.

"No idea, Jeff. Even that bird of his reckoned that he never had birthdays. I reckon, he must be in his early thirties though. Shall we just try a year – let's say 1983. That would make him thirty-two or thirty-three which I reckon would be about right."

"You are the one who should know, Sarge – know what I mean?"

He grinned at her to rob the words of any sting and Hilary felt herself flushing again.

"Get on with it, PC Maddox. We haven't time for that sort of nonsense now."

"Sorry Sarge; just a joke."

Maddox keyed in a series of blank spaces, then finished up with 1983 before turning back to the sergeant.

"Height?"

Hilary smiled with some relief. At last there was something she could give with reasonable accuracy.

"Six foot I reckon and his eyes are green."

He keyed the details into the computer then pressed another button and leaned back in his chair.

"Okay, let's see what this wanked out fruit machine coughs up. I'll bet a pound to a pinch of shit that there is nothing on McConnel."

"I hope you are right Jeff, but I still reckon Wemyss is too good a witness to be so wrong."

"The bugger is too good to be true, Skip. Who ever notices that much about someone in a casual conversation?"

"Here we go." Hilary interrupted him and pointed to the computer screen. Words and sentences began to appear and Hilary squinted at the flickering green characters.

"Fifteen suspects," she muttered and waited while the machine went on to detail all the men named McConnel who were known to police and had criminal records or were wanted for something. There were Allans, Alans and Alberts, but none with the forenames Alexander Herbert and Hilary felt an unreasoning disappointment. Maddox smiled at her in triumph.

"Told you see. Whatever else he might be, McConnel is no petty villain – know what I mean?"

"Hang on, Jeff. We haven't done yet. Let's try names that sound like McConnel. Perhaps he spells it differently."

Maddox' fingers flickered over the keys again and after a pause, more names and personal details appeared, this time with all those whose names sounded vaguely like McConnel. There were a number of them and the machine spewed out personal details of McCulloughs, McCauleys, McCrackens and one McConagle.

It was the last entry that suddenly transfixed them both.

"There you are, Jeff. Alexander Herbert no less and there is a Special Branch marker on him too. Can we find out any more?"

Maddox frowned.

"Dunno Sarge. Those markers usually mean no access to anyone else. Let's get one of the operators across and see if they can access it."

Two minutes later, a slim young man wearing a jacket and tie had taken Maddox' place at the console. He too looked doubtful when Hilary told him what they needed, but like most young men in the station, Malcolm Withers had fallen under the blonde sergeant's spell and would have walked on water for her, had he been asked. As he played with the keys, Hilary felt a curious sense of excitement in her chest. It was tempered with anxiety at what she might find out about McConnel though. There were very few people listed in the national computer with Special Branch markers beside their names and what the marker meant was that the security services had a specific interest in the man or woman named. They were invariably listed to discover their whereabouts and whatever the reason for his inclusion, the marker made McConnel – if he was indeed McConagle and the forenames seemed very coincidental – a great deal more important than a run of the mill housebreaker or dope-eating drop out.

His fingers moving at blistering speed, Withers pressed another selection of keys and the screen went blank for a moment. All three of them peered intently at the dark perspex and none of them were aware of the coiled up tension in their respective bodies. They were totally absorbed in the computer screen and none of the three was even aware of the room around them – the crackle of radios, the subdued him of telephones and the voices answering them, the everyday hustle and bustle that is an integral part of any busy police control room. Sergeant Hilary Bedwell, PC Jeff Maddox and the young radio operator were completely involved in what they were doing and for all of them, the moment carried a strange excitement of its own.

'McConagle, Alexander Herbert;' the screen flashed up the name in its distinctive green lettering. 'White male; six foot; dark hair: green eyes: born 6th December 1980 in County Antrim, Northern Ireland. No previous convictions recorded, but subject is of interest to Department SO12 (B) New Scotland Yard.'

Hilary racked her memory for details learned on her Bramshill course. If she remembered rightly, SO12 (B) was that part of Special Branch involved with the troubles in Northern Ireland. Yet those troubles were said to be over. What could Special Branch possibly want with a man like McConnel? She glanced back at the screen.

'In the event of subject coming to light,' it urged her formally, 'no attempt is to be made at approach or arrest. This department to be notified immediately. Officer in case D/C/I Turner.'

The entry told them nothing further and both men looked at the blonde sergeant. Hilary gnawed at her lower lip, a small frown puckering her brow as she wondered what to do.

Could this possibly be McConnel? The unusual Christian names certainly seemed too much of a coincidence and if the subject was a little older than her own estimate of McConnel's age, it was close enough to fit. The height and eye colour were identical and somehow she knew in her bones that Alexander Herbert McConagle would turn out to be the same man as her own smelly hippy who called himself only McConnel.

"What do you want me to do, Sarge?"

Malcolm Withers was looking at her expectantly and Hilary brought herself back to the present.

"I can ask CRO for a print out with more details, but that might bring Special Branch down on your neck, wanting to know what is going on. I take it this is the bloke you have in the frame for Thursday Joe?"

It was Maddox who muttered an agreement and Hilary thought a moment longer before coming to a decision.

"Do that please, Malcolm. Let's get as much detail as we can and I want a full print out please."

He turned back to the machine.

"Do you want the details telephoned through or sent by post, Sarge?"

"The post will do. It should only take a day or so."

As he bent back to the keyboard, Hilary rose to her feet and patted him on the shoulder.

"Thanks for your help, Malcolm. It was really appreciated."

Still frowning and obviously lost in thought, Sergeant Hilary Bedwell left the control room with Jeff Maddox limping behind her and in complete silence, they made their way back to her office.

"It doesn't make much sense, Jef,." she said at last. "How can a man like McConnel be of interest to Special Branch or any other security service? He has such an obvious contempt for everything that smacks of normal society and I cannot imagine him wanting anything to do with any official body."

"Perhaps that is why, Sarge. McConnel is no fool and maybe he has done something to worry the Ghostly Ones. Perhaps…"

He stopped and frowned, while Hilary shook her head as the same thought occurred to her. McConnel might be a drop out and even a petty housebreaker, but he surely wasn't a terrorist.

***

In the event, Hilary didn't have to wait the necessary two days for her print out to come through. She had only been back at her desk for thirty minutes when the telephone rang at her elbow.

Tearing her attention away from the file on Thursday Joe, she had been half heartedly reading while her mind wrestled with the McConnel problem, Hilary picked up the receiver.

"Sergeant Bedwell."

"Good morning, Sergeant Bedwell." The man on the other end of the line sounded brusque. "I am Detective Chief Inspector Turner from SO 12 at the Yard."

"Good morni…" She began but he cut her off.

"Sorry Sergeant – I don't have time for pleasantries. You did a PNC check on one Alexander Herbert McConagle a short while ago – is that correct?"

"Yes Sir."

"I have spent the last twenty minutes looking into your background, Sergeant Bedwell," he went on surprisingly. "You are obviously destined for high places, but I can see no reason at all for your interest in a man like McConagle.

'However, you made the check, so presumably he must have come to your notice somehow. I am not going to ask for an explanation over the phone, but I have someone already on his way down to see you. He should be there in about…." He paused and she could imagine him looking at his watch. "an hour and forty minutes from now.

'Make sure you are available please, Sergeant. If you have any problems with your superiors, refer them to me."

"But Sir…" She began and there was a squeak in her voice.

"No questions please, Miss. Detective Inspector Keenan will tell you all you need to know when he gets there In the meantime, I don't want you to discuss the matter with anybody. Is that understood?"

122

"Yes Sir." Hilary said meekly and the dialling tone told her that the Scotland Yard man had hung up on her.

Slowly replacing the receiver in its rack, Hilary turned back to the file on her desk, but the words were blurred before her eyes. Confusion and doubt swirled together in her mind.

Could McConnel be the same man as Alexander Herbert McConagle? Half of her hoped that he was, if only so that she could find out more about him. The other half prayed that she had it all wrong. McConagle, whoever he was, was obviously a great deal more than a footloose Cotswold hippy and she was not sure that she wanted to know too much.

In spite of DCI Turner's admonition, she rang through to the constables' report room and summoned Jeff Maddox.

"I'll meet you in the canteen for a cup of coffee, Jeff." She said briefly. "There have been developments in the McConnel business."

CHAPTER THIRTEEN

"I'm tellin' you, Sergeant Hilary, I 'aven't seen 'im since yore last visit like."

"I have to speak with him as a matter of urgency, Ellie."

Hilary Bedwell glanced at her watch. Time was getting on and she had to be back at the station when the detective inspector from the Yard arrived. It had been Maddox' idea to pay a quick visit to the Beacon and see whether McConnel had reappeared, but it seemed that it was a wasted trip.

"I have to know where he is, Ellie. It is vitally important to all of us."

"I'm telling you Miss, I don't know." The words came out in a wail and tears sprang to the girl's puffy eyes. "I've bin worried sick, Sergeant. 'Onest I 'ave. This isn't like 'im at all see."

In spite of her deep-seated antipathy toward the girl, Hilary knew she was telling the truth and felt her heart go out to her. Stepping forward, she put one hand on a thin shoulder and Ellie immediately burst into anguished sobbing.

"Is 'e in trouble, Miss?"

Hilary's feelings struggled between concern for the girl and the exigencies of her duty. If McConnel knew why they were looking for him, he would disappear for good, but she couldn't lie to this pathetic little creature and thereby add to her misery.

"He could be, Ellie. We don't know for sure which is why we need to speak with him."

Behind her, Jeff Maddox watched wordlessly, a huge, dark-clad bulk in the foetid confines of the bus. Somewhat to Hilary's surprise, Maddox seemed as reluctant to believe that McConnel was wanted by Special Branch as he had in the man being Thursday Joe.

"Never in a million years, Skip," he scoffed when she told him about the call from DCI Turner. "I know a serious villain when I see one and no matter

124

what the Shadows in the Factory might say, McConnel is just an ordinary bloke and certainly no terrorist suspect – know what I mean?"

Ellie snuffled against Hilary's shoulder and the sergeant wryly wondered what sort of a mess she was making of the starched tunic.

"I was scared tha' you lot 'ad nicked 'im see and weren't tellin' me. I've 'ardly slept since 'e left, I'm tellin' you."

Hilary tried to reassure her but wasn't sure that her words were having the desired effect.

"We aren't sure that he is the one we want, Ellie, but he might be. He has helped me in the past and I want to make sure he gets an opportunity to explain himself before we do anything more."

"I thawt 'e was grassin' to you Miss, I really did." Ellie said grimly and pulled herself back from Hilary's grasp. "It ain't like 'im at all, but 'e 'asn't been 'isself lately so I don't spose it surprises me like."

Yet again Hilary felt the familiar stab of jealousy at the girl's obvious personal knowledge of McConnel. Struggling to keep it down, she looked into the pinched, puffed face and again used her own handkerchief to wipe away the tears. Before she could say anything else, Maddox rumbled a question.

"What does he do on Thursday afternoons, Girl?"

For a long moment there was silence in the bus as Ellie tried to think out the question and the two officers waited for her answer. Her face screwed up in thought, she looked a little blank, then turned to Maddox with an eager look on her face.

"'E runs the market stall of course. Wot d'you fink 'e does?"

Maddox held up a hand in semi apology but continued his questioning.

"Every Thursday?"

"Of course." She said hotly. "I got my 'ands full with the kids see and market days are Thursday, Friday and Saturday like."

"Who did it yesterday?" Hilary put in quickly and the girl turned back to her.

"I did of course. I dunno where 'e is, so I left Lisa with Red and took the baby with me. Someone's got to keep the stall goin' see or we'll starve like. Wot is this, Sergeant? Why are you all so intrested in the stall all of a sudden?"

Ignoring the question, Hilary waited for Maddox to continue.

"Who is doing it today then, Lass? It is Friday and I presume it is business as usual – know what I mean?"

Ellie scowled at him.

"Yore tryin' to trap me ain't you? Make me say somefing wrong so I'll drop 'im in the shit like. Well yore not goin' to, see. I got Spike and Robbie to go down in my place. I couldn't find 'em yesterday, but they're always quite 'appy to 'elp me out when I need an 'and like.

'McConnel's a good man, Miss," she went on inconsequentially. "'E looks after us so well see an' I don't want anyfing to 'appen to 'im. I thawt 'e'd walked out on us last time you came up ere see, but if you 'aven't nicked 'im, then 'e must 'ave gone and dun it this time.

'Oh please find 'im for me, Sergeant Hilary."

Throwing her arms around Hilary, Ellie gave way to anguished sobbing and Hilary absently patted her shoulder.

"Alright Ellie Dear, we'll leave you in peace for the moment. If you do see McConnel, please impress upon him that this is urgent and I must speak to him."

Even as she said the words, Hilary felt the guilt of betrayal squirm in her belly. Feeling very Judas-like, she looked hard at the girl.

"If you hear anything, Ellie, I want to know straight away. Anything at all and I mean that. It really is terribly important."

Moments later, they were on their way back to the station and Hilary felt grimly despondent.

"Nothing seems to make sense, Jeff," she said to the big constable. "If McConnel isn't the bloke SO12 are after, then who in hell is he and where does he come from?"

"I don't know, Sarge, but I do know that he isn't Thursday Joe – know what I mean? He just isn't that sort, even if he is a scrote."

**

Once the two officers had gone, Ellie settled down to feed the baby. Her next visitor was completely unexpected and she started at the quiet footfall in the doorway. Her eyes lit up and she uttered a little cry when she saw who it was.

"McConnel," she breathed and his heart twisted inside him at the obvious delight in her voice. "Where 'ave you bin?"

"Out and about," he said laconically. "What did the coppers want?"

He had been on his way home when he spotted the police car in the clearing and had watched from the trees until Hilary Bedwell and her burly escort drove away.

"You." Ellie told him shortly. A little of her normal acerbity returning. Somewhat sadly, McConnel reflected that at one time she would have flung herself into his arms after an absence, yet now she merely carried on with what she was doing and waited for him to make any affectionate move.

"They wanted to know where you was and wot you do on Thursdays."

"Thursdays?" He looked puzzled. "Why Thursdays?"

Ellie scowled at him.

"I fawt you might be able to tell me tha', McConnel. I told 'em you was always on the stall like, but they didn't seem to believe me. Wot 'ave you bin up to now?"

But McConnel didn't appear to have heard her. A frown creased his forehead and he was lost in thought. With an obvious effort, he brought his attention back to the girl.

"What? Oh – nothing at all My Love. You know that Thursday is market day. How could I have been doing anything untoward?"

"They seemed really worried about it." She went on spitefully. "Even yore girlfriend reckoned you might be in trouble."

"She is hardly my 'girlfriend.'" His protest was automatic. "I wonder what is going on."

"You 'ad better go on an' ask her like." Her pale eyes flashed venom at the hippy. "P'raps she's worried cos she 'asn't seen you for a while like. Of course, I 'aven't see you neither, but I don't suppose that matters so much to you, does it?"

McConnel looked pained and moved across the bus towards her. As he bent to kiss her mouth, she turned aside so that his lips merely brushed her cold cheek. He stood up straight again and there was a deep sadness in his eyes as he gazed down at her and the baby. Ellie looked up defiantly.

"When they come again, do I tell 'em you was 'ere?"

"You do what you feel is best Ellie Dear." He said softly. "I will be back when I have found out what is going on."

"Don't bother McConnel," she snapped. "Go to your fancy piece like and leave us alone. We ain't no good for the likes of you anyway."

He paused at the door and looked across at Ellie for a long moment, his face sombre and the green eyes strangely dulled. Then he was gone and Ellie dropped her head into her hands and sobbed as though her heart was breaking.

***

Detective Inspector John Keenan was hardly the archetypal police officer – even from Scotland Yard where they sometimes tend to the unconventional.

In his mid twenties, the DI was painfully thin and hardly looked solid enough for the hurly burly of police life. He was dressed in patched jeans, a striped, collarless shirt and a leather jacket. He had black hair down to his shoulders and wore wire-rimmed spectacles that did little to disguise the bright curiosity in his eyes.

Having introduced himself to Hilary, he pulled a hard-backed chair up to her desk, turned it around and sat with his arms across the back support.

"Right, Sergeant Bedwell," he smiled at her but his eyes were hard,' "tell me why you want to know about the worthy Alexander Herbert McConagle."

Sitting back in her chair, Hilary took a moment or two to get her thoughts together. The unconventional appearance of her visitor had taken her by surprise and she struggled to look on him as any other officer, senior to herself. She had been expecting someone older, probably heavily built, wearing tweeds and bucolically smoking a large pipe. Keenan looked like any street corner tearaway and he had the easy confidence of a man who knew that he was good at what he was doing. He didn't appear to be much older than she was and had to be an exceptional policeman to be a DI at that age. She knew that she would have to be very careful with what she said to him. Taking a deep breath she plunged into her story.

Speaking in quiet, unemotional tones, she told the detective how she had come to meet McConnel and the strange effect, the man had had on her. She told him of the Beacon commune and the squalor in which they lived.

"What does he look like?" Keenan cut in at one point and Hilary paused in some confusion.

"It is actually quite hard to be sure, Sir. He wears a huge beard and his hair covers what little of his face is visible."

"Come on, Sergeant. You can do better than that. They must have taught you all about descriptive accuracy at Bramshill. You were on the Special Course, were you not?"

Hilary flushed at the softly spoken rebuke and mention of the police college. Furrowing her forehead, she tried to picture McConnel in her mind.

"Tall and thin I suppose, Sir, although he seemed extremely strong." She explained the marks left on Jeff Maddox' wrist and Keenan nodded sagely without saying a word.

"His hair is a sort of dark brown colour, although it is so matted and dirty that it is difficult to be sure. He has a slightly hooked nose and his eyes…."

Hilary paused, remembering the almost hypnotic effect that McConnel's emerald gaze had on her. Keenan said nothing, but she was aware that he watched her intently.

"His eyes are a strange, green colour. Very dark at times like pools of very deep water, yet they seem to change with his mood like the skin of a chameleon. When he is angry, they are so pale that they look almost white."

She was immediately aware of the relief in her visitor's face and the fact that tension seemed to drain from his shoulders.

"Okay Sergeant B," he said with friendly formality, "I am not sure what is going on as yet, but I am satisfied that your man McConnel is my Alexander Herbert McConagle. There cannot be two people in this world with eyes like that.

'Go on with your story please."

He stretched his long body and put his hands behind his head, still watching Hilary intently. For her part, she continued speaking with calm authority. She told of the information McConnel (she couldn't think of him as anything else) had given her and the beating he had received at the hands of Jeff Maddox.

"That was indirectly my fault," she admitted and he raised his eyebrows. "I laid into PC Maddox verbally on two occasions and each time it was in front of McConnel. I don't think Jeff appreciated that, but it was inexperience on my part."

DI Keenan smiled again.

"We all make mistakes Sergeant. As long as you are man enough to admit them, you'll be alright."

She couldn't help smiling at the latent sexism of the remark, but he seemed unaware of it so she went on with her story.

She told him about Ellie and her antagonism toward the police. She described the old red bus and the little chapel inside. Keenan smiled reminiscently, although this time he refrained from comment.

Hilary went on to describe McConnel's market stall and – a little hesitantly – explained how she had agreed to have coffee with the bearded hippy. The man from Scotland Yard grinned mischievously.

"That must have caused a stir in this uptight little community," he murmured. "Bright young police sergeant gallivanting with an awful low life like that – and on a busy Friday morning too. I can just imagine the rumours that must have flown about after that little episode. It's a wonder you weren't excommunicated on the spot."

Ignoring his facetiousness, she told him about the gunning down of PC Maddox and McConnel's competence in dealing with the injured leg. He nodded while she described the scene, but didn't say anything.

"He was marvellous, Sir," she went on. "I don't think I would have coped without him there and Jeff Maddox certainly would not be back on duty now without McConnel's expertise. Strangely, I think the two of them have almost become friends since that incident. Jeff won't hear a word against him."

"And you, Sergeant? How do you feel about McConnel now?"

Hilary shrugged wordlessly. If she was honest with herself, she didn't know the answer to Keenan's question. She missed McConnel and longed to see him again, but if he did turn out to be Thursday Joe, she knew she would be bitterly angry at his betrayal.

"I don't know Sir. I haven't seen him since that day, although I have a feeling that Jeff Maddox has."

"Okay, I will speak with PC Maddox in due course. Go on with your tale, Sergeant."

"There isn't much more to tell Sir. Chief Inspector Bolton was very disapproving of my relationship, such as it was with McConnel and one day he called me in and showed me a file that certainly seems to show that the man is one of our most notorious house breakers."

Hilary tried to describe her own feelings when she read Wemyss' statement, but Keenan was frowning heavily and didn't appear to hear her.

"That doesn't make sense, Sergeant Bedwell. I know Ally McConagle better than most and I cannot see him stooping to petty crime, no matter what the circumstances were."

"That was what PC Maddox said," Hilary told him. "But the description fits McConnel to a T. There cannot be two people in this area who look like he does."

She went on to explain how the witness had actually stopped to speak with Thursday Joe and with an air of subdued triumph, she produced a drawing from the papers on her desk. It had been delivered to her only minutes before Keenan's arrival and for her, there could be no doubt. It was McConnel staring out at her from the identifit poster and she felt mixed emotions stir in her belly whenever she looked at it. Keenan glanced briefly at the drawing, but remained unconvinced.

"That is McConnel, Sir," she said quietly as he returned the drawing. "There is no doubt about it I'm afraid."

"Very pretty, Sergeant, but it could almost be any damned crusty this side of The Smoke. It doesn't look too much like the McConagle I know."

Hilary bit back the questions that fought for prominence in her mind and concentrated on her story. The DI listened intently as she described both visits to Ellie and frowned at the news that McConnel had disappeared.

"I wonder where the bloody fool has gone now," he said softly but she knew he wasn't talking to her. "If he disappears again, we will never find the bugger."

Hilary could control her curiosity no longer and leaned forward across her desk. The youthful detective inspector returned her gaze and she could read nothing from his expression.

"Who is McConnel, Sir?" She asked earnestly. "What has he done to make him so important to you? Why don't you think he is Thursday Joe?""

"So many questions, Sergeant Bedwell," he sighed. "And no real answers to any of them."

They gazed at each other in silence for two long minutes. Hilary was determined that her visitor would not be allowed to avoid the issue. She had to know more about McConnel if she was going to find him. She had to know more if she was to cope with her strangely ambivalent feelings toward the man. She wanted so desperately to believe that he was not a criminal, but her instinct told her that she was in for a disappointment. The artist's likeness was too exact and although the evidence was all circumstantial, there was too much of it for there to be any mistake. McConnel or McConagle – whatever he wanted to call himself – was Thursday Joe. There could be no getting away from that, no matter what anyone said.

Keenan came back from his thoughts and rubbed his chin reflectively. When he looked across the desk at Hilary, his expression was bland but his eyes were sharp.

"You are a very good officer, Sergeant Bedwell. Your record is excellent and my own impressions confirm it."

"So everyone keeps telling me," Hilary cut in and there was so much bitterness and anger in her voice that Keenan looked momentarily taken aback. "'The first female Commissioner,' they say but what the hell does that mean, Inspector? I've had one man badly beaten up through my own lack of man management and then I find myself falling for a real toe rag of a crusty who turns out to be a villain who has been running rings around us for well over a year.

'You can imagine how that leaves me feeling, Mr Keenan. I am sure you could help if you wanted to, but when I try to regain a little of my self respect, you fob me off with the same soft-soap nonsense, I hear from everyone else.

'If it wasn't for me, Sir, you still wouldn't know where your man McConagle or whatever he bloody calls himself is, so surely I deserve to be told something?"

Detective Inspector Keenan looked with some compassion at the angry young sergeant and covered his own uncertainty by lighting a cigarette that he took from his jacket. He didn't offer the pack to her and she watched him coldly as he blew a perfectly symmetrical smoke ring at the ceiling.

"Your McConnel made a big impression on you, did he?"

For a moment, Hilary was tempted to deny it, but the denial would prove nothing, especially not to herself. Falling in love with McConnel might well do irreparable damage to her career prospects, but she had to know more about him and besides, it was probably too late anyway. Don Bolton did not approve and as Keenan had intimated, the story of her coffee date with the hippy would surface again and again, long after his saving of Jeff Maddox' leg had been forgotten. There was nothing she could do about any of it now, even had she wanted to.

Wearily, she nodded at the detective inspector.

"He is hardly 'my McConnel' Sir, but yes he did. I thought there was one hell of a fine man beneath that smelly exterior of his, but I was wrong wasn't I? He is just a petty villain like all the rest of them. Just another fucking useless crusty who made a fool of a gullible woman."

Ignoring her outburst, Keenan regarded her seriously for a moment.

"And he really does attract you physically?"

In spite of her anger, she couldn't help giggling, but the detective inspector didn't seem to consider his question in any way unusual.

"The first time I was close to him, I nearly gagged." She told him. "He smells of sweat, wood smoke, pot and general decay. He really is a horrible specimen and I tried to stay as far away from him as I could.

'It was only later when I started talking to him properly that I saw past the hippy image. He seemed so strong; so wise and…" she hesitated, then went on in determined tones, ".. yes, so damned lonely. I could see it in his eyes and it made me want to put my arms around him for comfort."

She shook her head and Keenan remained quiet, waiting for her to get it all out.

"There was definitely some strange form of empathy between us from the start and he obviously fancied me as a woman. I am not really used to that, Sir and it should have filled me with disgust, but such is McConnel's charm that I couldn't help responding. I still think about him at night, Sir and wonder how I would cope with him as a lover. As you can tell, they are hardly official thoughts."

Smiling slightly, he shook his head and waited for her to continue.

"Yet even if he is not Thursday Joe, there could never be anything like that between McConnel and me. You know that, Mr Keenan. The police service would never allow it. I don't suppose McConnel would give a tuppenny damn about that, but I have a career that I love and we both know that the powers-that-be would never stand for me having any sort of relationship with a man like that. Nothing might be said, but my promotion prospects would disappear and I would serve out my time as uniformed sergeant in some forgotten country nick where I can't do any harm. It isn't fair, but that is how the system works."

She sighed aloud but Keenan's saturnine face gave nothing way and she continued slowly.

"That doesn't stop me thinking about it though and wondering how it might be if we were allowed to be together. McConnel has something about him that captures my emotions and yes, damnit, he does attract me physically, even though I know nothing about him and nobody seems willing to tell me."

There was another silence and after searching briefly for an ashtray, Keenan ground out his cigarette on the floor with a neatly booted foot.

"You are out of your depth, Sergeant Bedwell." He told her not unkindly. "I started trying to explain a few moments ago, but you jumped down my throat.

'As you said yourself, McConagle – no, let's call him McConnel – is a hell of a man. I have known him for many years and fully agree with your assessment of his character, but as you rightly point out, your lives are so very different. He could never conform to your ambitions and the best thing you can do is forget all about him."

"How can I do that when I am leading a full scale operation to put him behind bars for God's sake?"

Her voice was almost a screech and Keenan looked at her with genuine compassion. When he spoke again, his tone was gentle and she could sense that he was trying to make things easier for her.

"You and I live and work in different worlds, Hilary, even though we are nominally part of the same organisation. My world is one of death and destruction – hardly common events in the life of a county plod."

"And McConnel is part of your world, Sir?"

"Leave out the 'Sirs' Girl. In spite of the rank, I am not used to that. I am John and you are Hilary. Okay?"

She nodded and he went on.

"Yes, I am very much afraid that McConnel has far more in common with me than he does with you. He might be a New Age type or whatever they call themselves at the moment, but he hasn't always been part of that particular fraternity."

He paused and in the silence, Hilary was suddenly aware of normal life going on in the building around her. Somewhere down the corridor, a sergeant shouted for more tea and the crackle of a police radio sounded from outside her window. Computer keyboards clattered from the secretarial pool and a fly buzzed irritatingly in one corner of the room. Somehow they all seemed part of another world – a world she had temporarily left behind.

"Please tell me about him, Sir – John," she asked the long haired man in front of her. "I really have to know."

He shook his head and the elegant curls danced in a beam of sunshine from the window.

"I can answer few of your questions, Hilary I'm afraid." He admitted wryly. "What I can tell you is that you won't catch him even if he does turn out to be your housebreaker. Ally McConagle is vastly experienced at avoiding people who are after his blood. Now, is there somewhere in this hick town of yours where we can get something to eat?"

She nodded eagerly.

"Yes of course, but won't you tell me first who McConnel really is?"

He laughed softly.

"You really are a persistent wench aren't you, Sergeant Hilary? I can see why our man was so interested.

'Tell you what; there are too many listening ears in any nick. Show me a place where we can get a reasonably decent steak and I will try and tell you a little – and I mean a little, Hilary Bedwell – more about McConnel."

It was when the steak had been served, his rare and hers medium rare, that he finally went back to the subject they had left in the office. The restaurant was almost empty and he had carefully chosen a corner table where they were unlikely to be overheard. Once the wine had been sniffed, tasted and poured, Keenan took a sip from his glass, swilled it around his mouth and swallowed with the air of a connoisseur.

"Lovely stuff," he commented with a smile. "It is surprising how many of these little, out of the way places have a wonderful cellar. Fortunately for those of us who appreciate the grape, the general public are far too accustomed to their cheap supermarket plonk and so the genuine article often goes undetected for years – which of course, usually makes it all the more delectable."

"I would never have taken you for a snob, Sir – John."

Hilary was almost jumping up and down in her seat. She wished the stupid man would stop burbling about wine and tell her something about McConnel, but he obviously intended to make her wait. Keenan smiled at her barely concealed impatience, but there was little humour in his eyes. Having carefully masticated a delicately cut slice of his steak, he leaned across the table and looked into Hilary's eyes. When he spoke, the words seemed

135

to fall into the space between them like stones dropped deliberately into a pool of water.

"Alexander Herbert McConagle," he told her without preamble, "is a long way from being your normal everyday crusty. His father made a fortune in the city somewhere and Ally was brought up on an Irish country estate with all the privileges afforded to children of the very rich. You know the scene – servants to make the beds and clean the shoes, a private education at Malvern College and then on to Oxford, plus all the little bits and pieces that go with being among the upper echelons of society in this class-ridden country of ours. Dad went into politics when he retired and with his connections, did bloody well for himself, to end up as Defence Secretary in a former Conservative government. From there it was but a small step into the House of Lords. Ally McConagle hasn't spoken to him in years.

'Ally himself is a serving member of the Special Air Service, believe it or not. You know – the 'who dares wins' lot, although he never took all that crap seriously. In spite of his education and background, he joined the army as an ordinary soldier and once he was accepted in the SAS, he worked his way up to the rank of captain. A man among men indeed. I suppose coming in on the ground floor so to speak, was his rebellion against the life he had been forced to live, but believe me, he was one hell of an asset to the army.

'Most members of the great British public are unaware of it, but despite the Good Friday agreement and the blithe pronouncements of mainland politicians, the war in Ulster still goes on virtually unabated nowadays. It just isn't news any more, what with Al Qaeda, Daesh, the Middle East, Syria and the refugee crisis in Europe. Now of course, we have this Brexit nonsense disturbing and dividing the nation so the continuing 'Troubles' are ignored and forgotten. Besides, our revered leaders don't want too much of what goes on to become general knowledge, so newspaper editors are forced to toe the official line. It wouldn't do for us all to know that the peace deal was just so much political hogwash now would it?

'Anyway, Hilary Bedwell, I am getting on one of my soapboxes and you wanted to know about Ally McConagle. Well, he disappeared from an active service unit in Northern Ireland just over two years ago and in any other military outfit would have been posted as a deserter long since. The SAS don't look on things like that however and provided he can still pass the selection course, will take him back without any fuss, just as soon as he deigns to reappear.

'If he reappears of course and I have a feeling in my plumbing, that might depend on you."

Hilary sat numbly in her chair, the meal forgotten and the man across the table from her barely seen. A confused jumble of almost panicky thoughts squabbled for precedence in her mind. Her face had gone very white but she was not aware of it. John Keenan pushed her glass towards her and she drank the wine without tasting it.

McConnel an army officer? It was almost unbelievable, yet it made an obscure sort of sense. She remembered his air of quiet command and the way he seemed to naturally take charge in a crisis, just as he had done with Maddox' leg. On the other hand, how could such a filthy example of modern degradation ever have been part of an elite regiment? All she knew about the SAS was their public image and their reputation for deeds of daring, but it did not seem possible that a man like McConnel could be subject to the military discipline of a fighting unit. He did not seem the type.

John Keenan broke into her thoughts.

"Besides, Hilary Dear, not even the SAS can afford to lose a man like your McConnel. He was an outstanding soldier and in any other regiment he would have been looked upon as a national hero many times over."

"I wish you wouldn't keep calling him 'My McConnel." Hilary complained absently but he ignored the interruption.

"Ally did a lot of wet work in Northern Ireland. You know what that entails, don't you?"

She nodded but he went on to explain in any case.

"Wet work describes undercover and usually illegal ways to fight a war. It invariably entails violence and often murder. It is not a nice way to fight, but it is part of any war and very necessary to achieve results. Governments and the military establishment turn a blind eye to it, no matter what liberal ideals they might prattle on about in public.

'Anyway Ally McConagle volunteered to work on his own and would disappear for weeks at a time. God alone knows where he lived, but the results he came up with were always tremendous. All of us on the ground in Belfast regarded him with awe and on the back streets of Londonderry where such men are ten a penny, he was very much a hero, even though his face and identity were unknown."

"What sort of results did he bring in? I mean – was he killing people or what?"

"Occasionally targets would disappear completely, so I assume he did the necessary with them, but more often than not, he turned their loyalties around. How he did it, nobody knew but time after time, known hard cases would give themselves up and many of them even came to work for the security forces against their former buddies. For a long time, Ally was known as The Persuader among our own men and believe, me, it fitted."

"Did you work with him?"

His eyes seemed to lose focus and she realised that his thoughts were far away.

"It was a weird arrangement really. I was attached to the SAS in a Special Branch role and somehow became his control for eighteen months." He said briefly. "I was the only one who ever had contact with him, but most of the time I did not have a clue as to his whereabouts, nor did I ever ask him how he went about his work. It was all very much against the rules, but while we achieved results, nobody said a word."

Hilary felt a chill across her shoulders that had nothing to do with the weather. Suddenly she understood so much more about the man she knew as McConnel. She remembered his mocking manner and realised that it masked a hidden tension and wariness that must have resulted from the dangers of his former life. She remembered the lithe way he moved and his strength, as well as the fact that except when looking into her eyes, his own had never been still. Keenan's revelations explained so much, yet they did nothing to explain why such a man would turn to petty burglary, particularly when he came from a wealthy family. If his father was a rich man and a former Cabinet Minister, he surely could not have been short of money.

Hesitantly, she voiced her thoughts to the unconventional detective inspector.

"Why would he go in for long term burglary, John? Could he be craving excitement all of a sudden?"

"That is the easy answer, Girl. Whatever else he might have been – and McConnel's service record is frightening by any standards – he is not your Holy Joe. That I can guarantee."

"Thursday." Hilary corrected automatically and he frowned.

"What? Oh I see; okay Thursday Joe. I'll tell you something else and that is that even if he was, you have no chance of catching him if he doesn't want to be caught. All you will do is frighten him off for ever.

'Come on Hilary. You have hardly touched your food."

With the subject of McConnel obviously closed, Hilary concentrated on an excellent lunch and afterwards they walked back to the police station in companionable silence. Chief Inspector Bolton was coming out as they went in through the front door and Hilary smiled at her boss and made no attempt to introduce her companion. Bolton went off, shaking his head in considerable perplexity.

CHAPTER FOURTEEN

Jeff Maddox was tired. It had been a long day and his leg ached abominably. When Hilary Bedwell had gone off with the man from Special Branch, he had seized the opportunity to knock off for the day and was driving home, an old tweed jacket slung over his uniform shirt and a cigarette dangling from his mouth. He was looking forward to putting his feet up with a nice cold beer to sort out his mind.

Maddox was bewildered and confused. The strange set up between his sergeant and the man known as McConnel had upset him from the start, but he did not see how the hippy could be in the frame as Thursday Joe. As a vastly experienced copper, Maddox felt that he could tell a real villain from a long way off and for all his faults, McConnel just was not the sort to be a petty housebreaker. Nor was it possible that he was a terrorist. That just did not fit.

There was also the matter of the relationship that was so obviously developing between McConnel and his sergeant. That really worried Jeff Maddox. He had taken Hilary Bedwell under his wing and wanted her to do well, but to fall for a man like the unkempt hippy was just asking for trouble. The police service had always been a narrow minded and conservative organisation that frowned on almost any relationship, not blessed by the bonds of matrimony and any sort of sexual liaison between Hilary and McConnel would inevitably have drastic consequences for the young sergeant.

Pulling his private car to a halt at a road junction, Maddox sucked hard on the cigarette and was about to throw the end into the road when his eyes widened as the passenger door opened and the object of his thoughts slid into the seat beside him.

"Will you stop bloody sneaking up on me, McConnel," the big constable roared. "You will give me a ruddy heart attack – know what I mean? Anyway, what the fuck do you want? I suppose you know that half the force are out looking for you and the situation is knocking the shit out of my sergeant?"

Smiling disarmingly, McConnel slipped the seat belt around his shoulders.

"Just drive on, Maddox. I want to talk to you."

Automatically the bemused policeman did as he was told. Steering the car without thought, he took a side road out of town and at the first available lay by, he pulled in and switched off the engine before turning to face his silent companion.

"Right Man – explain yourself and by God you've got some explaining to do – know what I mean?"

"Why are your lot looking for me?"

The bearded hippy sounded genuinely interested and the policeman narrowed his eyes.

"You mean you don't know?"

"Of course I don't Man or I wouldn't be here now, would I? I saw you and the lovely sergeant speaking to Ellie and when I asked her what it was about, she reckoned that you were rabbiting on about Thursdays. What's it all about, Maddox? Even you can't think I am this housebreaking merchant I've read about in the local rag. Or do you?"

Jeff Maddox looked hard at his unexpected passenger and his voice was unusually serious when he spoke again.

"I don't personally think so, McConnel no, but others certainly do. Even your girlfriend is convinced and it is cutting her up – know what I mean?"

"Come off it, Maddox. You know I have nothing to do with that sort of nonsense surely? Why me of all people?"

Slowly and deliberately, Jeff Maddox took out his cigarettes. Carefully selecting one from the packet, he lit up, holding McConnel's eyes while the hippy looked back at him without speaking. Opening the window to let smoke filter from the vehicle interior, the policeman told McConnel about the witness who had described him so exactly and the artist's impression that was so incredibly lifelike.

"I tell you what McConnel, whether you did the jobs or not, you are stuffed out of sight anyway. That drawing was you to the life and Sergeant Bedwell is worrying herself bloody sick over it. If you aren't Thursday Joe, your best bet is to come back to the nick with me and let's try to sort it out – know what I mean?"

"I know what you mean alright, Maddox. I come in with you, get banged up and everyone is happy at a good result. Guilt or innocence on my part means nothing. It is all a question of the crime figures now.

'Who is this wonderful witness of yours anyway?"

"A man called Wemyss." Maddox told him shortly. "Respectable businessman type who lives on his own in Warburton Close. I tell you man, he had you bang to rights, even down to that scrofulous bloody hat you wear."

He paused at the sudden fierce light in McConnel's eyes, but any comment he might have made was forestalled by the hippy's next question.

"And you reckon Sergeant Hilary is taking it badly?"

"Of course she bloody well is, McConnel. The poor lass is gutted – absolutely fucking gutted. I don't know what she sees in you, but she certainly has the hots for you right now – know what I mean? The boss has put his own career on the line by putting her in charge of the operation so that she can prove herself to him, but that only makes things worse for her. The poor lass is totally mixed up and confused – know what I mean?

'Come on Man," he went on in a softer tone. "I'll take you in to the nick with me and perhaps you can persuade her of your innocence."

He reached for the ignition key and McConnel's hand snaked out to grip his wrist. The big man's eyes narrowed, but he remembered the strength in the hippy's wiry frame and made no move to resist.

"Listen Maddox, I am not going anywhere with you. You owe me one remember. As you said you got more than a little carried away and I am not going to forget how I came by these aches and pains in a hurry. I came to you, not only because you are a man I can talk to, but also because you alone can help Hilary Bedwell and by Christ she obviously needs your help.

"I will sort out your Thursday housebreakings for you, but I will do it on my own. In the meantime, I want you to ensure that Hilary Bedwell doesn't drop herself into any more trouble over me."

Jeff Maddox looked grim.

"Don't be an arsehole, Man. It isn't Hilary who is causing the trouble – it is you. She is a bloody fine copper – know what I mean. She also has a great future ahead of her provided she keeps her nose clean. You are the one who seems to be trying to fuck it all up for her."

McConnel nodded and there was a sombre look in his eye.

"I know that, Maddox. By God I know that and it worries me, but there is sod all we can do about feelings in this life. Somehow something pretty damned special has developed between Hilary and me, but I'm damned if I know what to do about it."

"Fuck all Man. There is fuck all you can do. Just get out of her life and leave her alone."

Maddox almost snarled the words and McConnel leaned back against the car door and looked at him with infinite weariness.

"Easy to say PC Maddox, but bloody hell to comply with. I had intended to slip out of her life and move on somewhere else. I might even have done so by now, but suddenly I have your damned housebreakings to sort out."

"Forget all that crap, McConnel. If it isn't you doing the Thursday jobs, then eventually Chummy will slip up anyway and you'll be in the clear. For the moment, just bugger off, Man and leave us all alone."

"I will certainly leave Hilary Bedwell alone," McConnel told him slowly. "But I will not allow my good name, such as it might be to be sacrificed for someone else. I will sort out your Thursday Joe for you and then we will see. In the meantime, you are still in charge of Hilary Bedwell's welfare and I expect you to look after her."

Although he spoke quietly, McConnel's eyes bored into Jeff Maddox and the expression in their depths was grimly serious. Maddox shifted uncomfortably in his seat and tried to cover the movement by stretching his injured leg out in front of him, but McConnel wasn't fooled. Taking one final lungful of nicotine from his cigarette, the big constable flung the butt out on to the road and turned once again to face his unorthodox passenger.

"Where are you going to be, McConnel?"

"Shit Man, you asked me that before and I don't really know," McConnel shrugged. "I will be looking out for Hilary's welfare, you can bet your sweet life on that, but you are the only one in a position to really help."

"What is it about bloody hormones, McConnel? Since you dropped into her life, my sergeant has been a quivering bloody wreck – know what I mean? I will help her all I can, you know that but with you around, none of us are going to get anywhere. She has to be allowed to concentrate on her job. Leave her alone, Man."

"Yeah I will Maddox and I know all about the hormone factor, believe me. For some reason, the girl makes my hormones work overtime too. I don't know what it is about her, but she has taken over my soul and I just want to be sure she is okay. As soon as I've sorted out your housebreaker, I will drop right out of her life, I promise you.

'In the meantime, you just make damned sure you keep her out of trouble. You owe me Maddox, we both know that, but this I want you to do purely for Hilary."

Maddox opened his mouth to make a point, but a steely look in the strange green eyes quickly subdued him and he took another cigarette from his pocket.

"As I think I told you once before, Jeff Maddox, you are a hard man," McConnel told him quietly; "but believe me, I am more than accustomed to dealing with hard men. You might not like that idea, but that is just tough. We have had our differences over the past few months and I feel the same about you as you probably do about me, but let's try and get on for Hilary's sake if nothing else."

Maddox smiled somewhat sourly and for a long moment, the two men locked gazes without a word being said. It was the policeman who eventually capitulated.

"Yeah, you are probably right, McConnel. You know, in different circumstances and if you weren't such an oxygen thief, I could almost like you."

The words sounded defensive and it was McConnel's turn to smile.

"Forget it, Maddox. We play by different rules, you and I, so let's continue as we are without worrying about likes and dislikes, shall we? Once I have sorted out your Thursday bloke, the slate will be clean between us. All I am asking is that the lovely Sergeant Bedwell has your full support and if she gets into trouble at any stage, you are there to back her up."

"Why are Special Branch interested in you, McConnel?"

The question caught the bearded hippy by surprise and he flashed a quick look at the policeman.

"Why should they be, Maddox?"

"I dunno Man, but there is something about you that is a long way from kosher and it worries me – know what I mean?"

In rumbling tones, he went on to tell his passenger about the search of the Police National Computer they had made and the Special Branch marker that had showed up beside the name of Alexander Herbert McConagle.

"After that enquiry, some big deal from the factory drove up specially to see the sergeant," he went on. "They are out somewhere now, so there must be something very wrong with you Man – know what I mean?"

McConnel listened in complete silence and a frown ruffled his forehead. When Maddox finished his story, the hippy shook his head in infinite weariness.

"Shit Maddox; that is all I bloody need. I'm not going to go into my relationship with the Branch, but take it from me, it has nothing to do with you or Sergeant Hilary Bedwell."

Again there was silence in the vehicle as the two men exchanged another long look. Moments later, McConnel slipped out of the car and disappeared into nearby fields. After sitting in silent contemplation for nearly five minutes, Jeff Maddox started the car and drove slowly and thoughtfully home. He was not at all sure what he was getting himself into.

***

"His problem has always been that he thinks too much."

The speaker was Detective Inspector Keenan and the subject under discussion was the man known to Hilary as McConnel. Left somewhat dissatisfied by the little she had learned about McConnel over lunch with the unorthodox man from Scotland Yard, Hilary had pleaded with him for more information.

"It means an enormous amount to me, Sir. Please don't leave me in suspense."

"John." Keenan corrected absently and after a moment of hesitation, he gestured toward a dilapidated old Citroen saloon, parked in one corner of the police yard. It had probably been beige coloured originally, but dents, rust and dirt had obscured much of the paintwork over the years.

"Hop into my rust bucket, Hilary and we will go for a drive where nobody can possibly hear what I have to say. Don't worry," he noticed the look of horror she bestowed on the ancient vehicle and had obvious difficulty in suppressing his smile; "she is not as bad as she looks and certainly won't break down on us."

In fact the vehicle had purred with the silky smoothness of a sewing machine and Hilary had the impression that a hugely powered engine lurked beneath the battered bonnet. She had shown Keenan where to go and once out of town, they had looked for a suitable spot to be alone. Now they sat on a bench overlooking rolling green hills and a patchwork kaleidoscope of green fields, separated by venerable stone walls. Sheep grazed in some of the fields, a skylark trilled in the middle distance and only the muted hum of distant traffic told them that the real world was still around them. Keenan sounded almost wistful as he went on.

"As I told you Hilary, he did a wonderful job in Northern Ireland. He was directly responsible for breaking up a number of terrorist cells and God alone knows how many people owe their lives to him.

'The trouble was that he took it all so damned personally. Ally McConagle seemed to carry the cares of the entire populace on his shoulders and it wore him down till he cracked. He was always a crusader at heart and looking back on it, I can only say that he was the wrong sort of man for that kind of war."

"But how can you say that now?" Hilary protested. "You have spent the last two hours telling me how good he was at the job."

The DI nodded thoughtfully but without enthusiasm.

"Oh he was, Hilary; he was incredible at it. There can be no doubt at all about that, but what it took out of him is another matter. In the long run, it probably destroyed him. I can sympathise with your fondness for the man because he is one hell of a character, but I do so wish it hadn't happened."

"If I hadn't fallen for him, you wouldn't know where he is now."

He laughed uproariously.

"That is rich, Hilary and you had better not let your bosses hear you. I still don't know where in hell the bugger is, but perhaps it might have been better if he had merely disappeared into his hippy lifestyle and been forgotten for ever. I shall be worried for him until we find him."

"You said we probably wouldn't." She reminded and he laughed again.

"I said you wouldn't, Sergeant Bedwell. I have a few more resources at my disposal, but I half hope that I don't get anywhere too. He is probably far safer in his own little world."

"Safer from what, Sir – John? Surely he can't come to harm in a place like this? Perhaps if I told the Boss about him, we could arrange some sort of protection if you really think he is in some sort of danger?"

Keenan turned to look at her and there was a spark of anger in his eyes.

"Oh no you don't, Sergeant Bedwell. I have already told you far more than I ought to have and it has to remain strictly between us. Your McConnel is a man who skates on very thin ice and the more people who know his identity, the more chance he has of catching a bullet in the teeth."

Hilary looked distinctly sceptical.

"Come off it John. This is the Cotswolds damnit! We don't have gangland type killings here."

Visibly agitated, the unorthodox Detective Inspector rose to his feet and looked down at Hilary. Although his tone was light when he spoke, his face was suddenly very bleak.

"I told you that Ally McConagle and I operate in a different world from yours Hilary, didn't I?"

She nodded mutely.

"Well, it is true, but your McConnel is very much part of my world. He might have escaped for the moment, but he can never get away from it entirely. His death would be of enormous propaganda value to many people and they wouldn't hesitate to kill him, wherever he might happen to be. That is why I feel it might have been better if his whereabouts had never come to light. The men who want McConnel dead have only to get a whisper that he might be in this part of the country and they won't hesitate to turn your smug little town into a battlefield."

Hilary felt her blood run cold at the seriously spoken words and wondered what she would do if McConnel was killed. For the moment, she had forgotten that he was a wanted man and she was in charge of the hunt for him.

"I won't say a word, John." She promised and Keenan nodded grimly before turning toward his car.

"It really could mean life or death for your McConnel, Sergeant Bedwell, believe me."

On that note, they drove in silence back to the police station and back in her office, the DI from Scotland Yard prepared to leave.

"Keep on with your operation, Hilary Bedwell and I hope you catch your Thursday break in merchant. It won't be Ally McConagle, but if you should hear the slightest whisper as to his whereabouts, I want to know immediately please. He is a very persuasive and charming man, so he will doubtless try to convince you otherwise, but remember what I said please. It is not only a matter of national security at stake, but it is also our friend's life on the line if anything goes wrong."

"Are you going to talk with PC Maddox, Sir?" Hilary felt the need to be formal now they were back on official ground. "He might well know where McConnel – or whatever his name is – might be."

"No, Sergeant," He was equally formal. "I have wasted too much time already, so I'll be on my way. You can talk with the worthy Mr Maddox and if he does know anything, you know what to do."

With that he was gone, and a very thoughtful police sergeant returned to her task of apprehending the criminal known only as Thursday Joe.

CHAPTER FIFTEEN

From the passenger seat of a gleaming white, BMW open coupé, Hilary Bedwell checked the disposition of her men against a clipboard, held on her lap.

The open sports car was hardly inconspicuous, but at least it wasn't likely to be taken for a police vehicle. It belonged to a junior constable who obviously had more money than was good for him and Jeff Maddox had commandeered it for the operation. The previous day, it had been fitted out with the necessary radio and communications equipment and the big fellow was obviously very pleased with his choice. She had originally asked him to produce suitably inconspicuous transport so that they would not be noticed and he had certainly come up with something out of the ordinary. He also seemed to have taken to his undercover role with enthusiasm.

Dressed in a tweed cap, checked shirt and aviator sun glasses, he lounged behind the steering wheel, a large cigar clamped between his teeth and his eyes flitting across the scenery while he listened to his sergeant speaking quietly into the radio handset.

Hilary herself bore little resemblance to the trim, uniformed police sergeant that he was accustomed to and Maddox hadn't been able to suppress a low whistle of approval when he first saw her ensemble.

Dressed in a blue jump suit with grey, braided piping, she had her blonde hair loose across her shoulders and looked as elegantly beautiful as any fashion model. White-framed dark glasses lent a touch of pure exotica to her appearance.

"What a handsome couple we make, Sergeant Bedwell," he murmured as she replaced the microphone beneath the walnut panelled dashboard. "Seems a pity to waste it don't you think? Why don't we leave the rest of them to it and make for the sea side – know what I mean?"

"You just concentrate on the job in hand, PC Maddox," she said severely, but there was a twinkle of amusement behind the shadowed lenses. "This is

149

the first time we have been given sufficient manpower for this little op and we are going to catch Thursday Joe today or heads will roll."

'Whose head would it be?' Maddox wondered to himself. It was Thursday afternoon and three days since his meeting with McConnel, yet he still found it difficult to believe that the encounter had actually taken place. For all his rough and ready methods, Jeff Maddox was a conscientious officer and he knew that he should have taken the hippy back in to the station for questioning. Instead of which, he had agreed to McConnel's suggestions and left him to make good his escape. It was a blatant dereliction of duty and the memory tugged uncomfortably at the big fellow's conscience. He hadn't dared to mention the meeting to Sergeant Bedwell and when he had asked her about her conversation with the detective inspector from Scotland Yard, she had been uncharacteristically reticent.

"I can't tell you much, Jeff I'm afraid. I've been sworn to secrecy and threatened with all sorts of nasty consequences if I open my mouth."

"You still think McConnel is Thursday Joe?"

She nodded mutely and there was a sheen of moisture in her eyes.

"Whether he is or not, we'll get Chummy today, Sarge, that's for sure," he murmured mildly although doubts flared in his brain. This was not the first time a major operation had been mounted to catch Thursday Joe and the man still seemed able to avoid the police with total impunity. Maddox prayed to a God he had almost forgotten that McConnel really wasn't the man they were looking for.

"At least we know what he looks like now." Hilary broke musingly into his thoughts. "Everyone has his description and if he is seen, he will be arrested immediately. Surely he can't get away from us again?"

Big Jeff Maddox wasn't quite so sure, but he kept his doubts to himself.

***

Two streets away from the spot where the sports car was parked, a dapperly dressed man, carrying a leather briefcase walked confidently up the front driveway of a big house, set well back from the road. In spite of the afternoon heat, he wore a dark suit, together with a neat grey trilby and looked like an insurance salesman or perhaps a Jehovah's Witness. Looking neither to left or right, he advanced toward a heavy front door and rapped peremptorily on the brass knocker.

There was no answer to his summons and after trying two more bursts of knocking on the door, the man wandered around the back to see if a window might have been left open. Three minutes later, he was back at the door and having produced a set of metal picks from one pocket, he set to work on the lock. A moment later, the door swung open and he disappeared inside, carefully pulling it closed behind him.

From the uppermost branches of a tall beech tree in one corner of the garden, McConnel watched and waited, a grim smile twitching on his lips.

***

"What worries me, Sarge," Maddox parked the sports car outside the gates of a small park, "is why you are so sure our Joe will do this particular village today?"

Two urchins gazed at the rakish little vehicle with interest, but both officers ignored them. Hilary smiled tightly at the question but made no effort to enlighten the big constable.

"Today is our day Jeff, I am sure of it. He will be here somewhere, you'll see."

Hilary tried to sound confident and prayed that she would be proved correct. There were thirty-three police officers deployed around the hill top village and her head would really be on the block if the exercise proved to be another waste of tax payers' money. Even Don Bolton had been sceptical.

"It seems an awful concentration of manpower, Sergeant," he had grumbled when she told him of her plans. "Surely it would be far better to spread them out a bit and cover a wider area?"

"No Sir." Hilary was adamant. "We have tried that so often and you know it doesn't work. We have to flood one particular area and hope that we have guessed correctly."

"Hope that you have guessed correctly, you mean," Bolton stressed the pronoun and was obviously unimpressed. "I might agree with you if we had something to go on, but why on earth do you think Chummy will target Enderleigh Bishop this week? Hasn't he been there before?"

"Yes Sir, but that was nearly a year ago and he got away with peanuts. I am sure he will want to improve his luck and there are a number of big houses in the village that he could have a go at."

"You sound very sure, Sergeant, but I just hope you are correct or we will both be on the carpet for wasting police manpower."

"I know that Sir, but I really do have a good feeling about this one," she smiled with a confidence that she didn't feel. "Call it feminine intuition if you like but I just know he will be there."

She couldn't very well tell the glowering Chief Inspector of the phone call she had received at home three evenings previously. The call that had set her pulses racing in spite of her confidence that McConnel was Thursday Joe. The deep, soft voice that always seemed able to reduce her knees to quivering weakness had murmured in her ear and she had listened in tremulous silence.

"I am ashamed of you, Sergeant Bedwell," McConnel began with a hint of his usual mockery. "You show a singular lack of faith sometimes, but I suppose I can't blame you. That drawing was very lifelike wasn't it?

'Try Enderleigh Bishop this Thursday."

He had said no more and the buzzing of the receiver told Hilary that he had hung up without waiting for her comments. She had found it difficult to sleep that might. Quite apart from the almost hypnotic effect of McConnel's voice, his words had left her confused and worried.

She knew the village of Enderleigh Bishop and it would certainly make a fine target for Thursday Joe, containing as it did, a number of secluded homesteads, most of them occupied by businessmen and politicians who spent most of their time in the city. Leafy avenues separated the houses and the entire area had an ambience about it of quietly contained opulence. With most of the houses having state of the art alarm systems, it was rarely targeted by burglars, but what would happen if McConnel was merely trying to lead her away from his real target? In spite of his honeyed words on the telephone and the open scepticism expressed by Jeff Maddox and DI Keenan, she still found it difficult to believe that McConnel was not Thursday Joe. Whenever her own doubts came to the fore, she had only to read the description given by the witness Wemyss or look at the artist's impression of the wanted man to be convinced that the bearded hippy had to be the man they were looking for.

None of it made sense, but in spite of her doubts and those of her superior officer, Hilary had focussed the entire surveillance operation on Enderleigh Bishop. Don Bolton had grudgingly given her his support and additional officers had been brought in from neighbouring districts. Plain clothes teams had been set up and surveillance sectors allocated to everyone involved.

Civilian cars equipped with police radio sets had been parked in strategic places and as the officer in charge of the operation, Hilary had given herself a patrolling brief with Jeff Maddox, himself still officially on light duties. Now everyone was in place and there was nothing left for her to do but wait.

"I hate to prove myself a chauvinist pig, Sarge," Maddox told her dryly; "but I have never had a great deal of faith in intuition – be it feminine or otherwise – know what I mean?"

Leaning right back in his seat, the big man took a comforting draw on his cigar and tipped the felt cap over his eyes. Hilary shifted uncomfortably in her own bucket seat. Her stomach was churning with nervousness and she wondered where Thursday Joe was at that moment.

CHAPTER SIXTEEN

The man in the dark suit moved swiftly though the house, his eyes darting around him as he assessed the best hiding places for loose cash. The ground floor was luxuriously furnished and much of the furniture looked extremely valuable, but he had no eyes for that. After trying a few drawers in what looked like an antique escritoire, he shook his head briefly. Few people kept portable valuables or cash in the more public sections of a dwelling and with another quick glance around, he ran up carpeted stairs in silence, born of much practice. Moving through an open bedroom door, he gasped in muted shock as he found himself face to face with the largest teddy bear he had ever seen. Grinning somewhat sheepishly at his own nervousness, he took a deep breath to steady himself and continued his search.

The main bedroom yielded unexpected surprises and a grin of extreme satisfaction spread across his face. In a battered suitcase, pushed carelessly under a king size double bed, he found nearly five hundred pounds in used notes and these he stuffed into various pockets before pushing the suitcase back under the bed. He worked with easy fluency and as soon as the money was safely stowed, looked around for more. A few pounds from a bedside cabinet and twenty more from the drawer of a cluttered dressing table made for an excellent afternoons work and with the money secure, he looked around him before turning for the door that he had left open behind him.

This time it wasn't a teddy bear that confronted him and he felt his legs freeze with shock as he gazed into the mocking green eyes of McConnel.

"Well, well, well;" the unorthodox hippy said in conversational tones. "What a surprise, Joey Boy. I heard on the grapevine that you had turned respectable, but I was obviously wrong wouldn't you think?"

"Ally McConagle," the trapped burglar gasped. "What the fuck are you doing here?"

"Looking for you I suppose. I don't like being blamed for other people's work, but I have to admit that was a pretty fair description you gave the Filth, Joey Boy. You had me down to a 'T' didn't you? Even put my hat in as a last

154

minute extra or so I'm told. Made it all the more convincing for the poor sods."

"I had to tell them something, Ally Man," the housebreaker said with an uneasy smile. "I was almost home after a good afternoon when I ran into a patrolling plod. I managed to distract him with that description, but if he had searched me, I'd have been done for."

"You are well and truly done for now in any case, My Friend. I am damned if I am going to carry the can for your shenanigans and besides, you have done my love life – such as it was – more bloody harm than even you could possibly imagine. That I will not forgive."

"There was nothing personal in it Ally, I promise you," the man's voice was a whine and he almost wrung his hands in his distress. "I had seen you in town that morning remember and you immediately sprang to mind when the Bobby was questioning me. I had to say something to put him off the scent. You can surely understand that?"

"I do, I do." McConnel said soothingly. "I suppose that as soon as that idiot plod was out of the way, you slipped around the corner and did the drum next door, just to make it all the more convincing?"

McConnel smiled and his tone was gently encouraging, but his eyes were savage as he looked at the cringing villain. The man nodded eagerly and seemed only too pleased to admit to the crime.

"I had to Ally. The bastard had me dead to rights and there was nothing else I could do. Hell Man, I can cut you in on all this. I make a damned sight better living from doing drums than ever I did as a soldier or a salesman. We can go halves on everything I get if you like."

"Noways Man; I am in enough trouble already. Anyway, I can't comment on your selling abilities Joey Boy, but you were certainly never cut out for soldiering. You seem to be a bloody good liar though and I do not appreciate being taken for a patsy."

"What are you going to do?"

The hesitantly asked question seemed to hang in the room for long seconds and McConnel hesitated before a big grin erupted behind his beard. The burglar visibly relaxed, but his shoulders straightened again at the hippy's next few words.

"Not me Joey Boy – it is you who has all the doing to do. You are going to tell all and get the Filth off my back or you and I are going to fall out quite seriously - again."

155

Fifteen minutes later, McConnel left the house by the front door. He was alone and smiling slightly as he slipped through the shadows of the garden. Behind him, the solid, Cotswold-stone walls gave no hint of the scene that had been enacted within.

***

Neither officer saw him approach. Maddox still had his cap tilted over his face and Hilary was restlessly scanning the surroundings, although she could not have said exactly what she was looking for. The first either of them knew of his presence was when the sports car lurched and McConnel leaped into the tiny rear compartment. Smiling somewhat enigmatically, he thrust his bearded face between them before either of them could move a muscle.

"I can see why the citizens of this county sleep so soundly in their beds at night," the deep voice dripped with sarcasm as he pressed a small, hard package into Hilary's hand. "Your plain clothes coppers stand out like a bunch of rapists in a nunnery and I don't suppose either of you can see a thing through those fancy shades, you're wearing. If I wasn't such a law abiding citizen, I might even consider a career in crime.

'Take that Sergeant Bedwell and you will find your villain at a house called The Elms in the next street but one."

Before either of them could react to what he said, he was gone, slipping out of the car and disappearing around a corner without ever once seeming to hurry. Eyes wide with shock, Hilary turned to look at her companion and he summed up the feelings of both of them in brutally succinct manner.

"Well I'll be fucked with a rusty tomato. That was a bloody surprise."

Hilary was equally nonplussed but after a momentary hesitation, she found her voice.

"Neatly put, PC Maddox and I quite agree, but perhaps we ought to get around to The Elms and see whether he was right."

"I reckon we might need back up, Sarge. McConnel didn't say whether this bloke is moving around or what."

"I don't think he needed to, did he?"

"No, probably not, but we had better call the support in anyway."

While Hilary spoke quietly to some of the closer teams, Maddox gunned the powerful sports car into life and grit and gravel spurted from under the rear wheels as they took off. To use the radio, Hilary had put McConnel's package down between them and Maddox picked it up as he drove. Inside loosely wrapped brown paper nestled a micro cassette recorder and the big constable grinned wolfishly.

"Fuck my dog and tell me about it," he muttered with vulgar vehemence. "The scruffy little sod has even given us the evidence."

CHAPTER SEVENTEEN

The flat was small, but it was hers and she loved it. The entire residence consisted of one comfortably spacious bedroom, a tiny lounge and both kitchen and bathroom, so minuscule that movements had to be thought out in advance if breakages were to be avoided. To Hilary, it was her home and her castle, while the fact that she owned it completely, more than made up for any discomfort. This was the one place in the world where she could escape from the stresses and strains of everyday life. Tastefully set out with furniture and art work, she had chosen herself, the flat was a haven of peaceful sanity where she didn't need to think about The Job and could spend her time reading, writing up her diary or listening to classical music. This was the place where a gentle young woman took the place of Police Sergeant Hilary Bedwell and she always felt a lift in her spirits when she entered the little flat.

She had neighbours of course, but they tended to keep to themselves and that suited Hilary. In spite of her good looks and the job she did, she was an introvert at heart and she invited few visitors to her refuge. Those who were allowed in, invariably came as friends rather than colleagues. Everyone at the station knew exactly how she felt and usually left her to herself except when it was unavoidable.

She frowned irritably to herself at the quiet knock on her front door. She did not feel like visitors. It had been a wonderful day and she had come home later than usual after celebrating their success with the other members of her team. The man Wemyss had been detained overnight, but only after giving a long and detailed statement describing many of the crimes for which he would eventually appear in Court.

Without waiting for the promised back up, she and Jeff Maddox had entered The Elms somewhat cautiously, the big constable going ahead of her so as to protect her with his bulk, although that had not been needed. They had found Wemyss awaiting their arrival in a well fitted kitchen. He had been firmly bound to a chair and she couldn't help wondering whether McConnel had chosen that room for the knives on view, which would only have added to the imprisoned man's torment. "Well, well, look what the cat's brought in." For once Maddox didn't add his usual 'know what I mean' and Hilary glanced at him in amused disbelief. "Who might you be, My Friend?"

The big man proceeded to interrogate the hapless captive without making any effort to loosen his bonds and the story he told them was a fascinating one. Without even searching his memory, he had remembered at least fifty house breakings in the area and once they found the loose cash, so carefully stowed around his person, there could be no question that his story was true. Hilary had no doubt that as soon as they had him back in the police station under proper interrogation, he would remember many more houses from which he had obtained his illegal income.

It wasn't long before other members of the team arrived on the scene and Maddox somewhat reluctantly released the dapper little man from his chair. He pushed him none too gently toward a waiting police car and two other officers bundled him unceremoniously on to the back seat. "Take him back to the nick, Fellas," Maddox boomed cheerfully to the patrol car crew. "He and I are going to have a cosy little chat in the morning – know what I mean?"

Back at the station, a PNC check had revealed the fact that Joseph Seward Wemyss was a former soldier with a long string of criminal offences chalked up against his name, both before, during and after his stint in the armed forces of Her Majesty. His arrest had been a major coup for Hilary and her team and it wasn't long before her telephone was ringing as officers from other police stations had come through with requests for information and queries as to when they too could interview Joe Wemyss.

The news had spread fast and both Don Bolton and Detective Inspector Hollis had put money behind the bar so that the team could celebrate their success in the customary manner. The party had been in full swing and the singing had only just started when Hilary slipped away and returned home to be alone with the confusion of her thoughts. Her feeling of total relief at McConnel's non involvement in the Thursday burglaries had been tempered by the knowledge that she was not likely to see him again. He would hardly be keen to further their relationship when she had been harbouring such grave suspicions about him. Had he not provided them with the man Wemyss himself, he might well have been the one languishing in police cells and she, Hilary Bedwell would have been entirely to blame.

Besides which, he had not been seen on the Beacon in ages and a telephone call to Detective Inspector Keenan that evening had elicited no more than a dry chuckle from the Special Branch Man.

"Well done Sergeant Hilary," he said. "That is a nice little result for you, although it doesn't make my job any damned easier. Our Boy will be over the hill and running now, mark my words. What a lousy coincidence that Joe Wemyss should be operating in your area."

"You know him then, Sir?"

"Oh yes, I know him alright and so does your McConnel. They worked together for a while in Belfast and our boy Ally was lucky to avoid a general court martial for beating Wemyss to within an inch of his useless life."

"What on earth for, Sir?"

"Wemyss was involved in some sort of shady deal even then, Hilary and Ally McConagle disapproved. A young girl died as a result of Wemyss' finagling and although nobody is quite sure of the details, he then spent nearly three months in hospital to ponder on his sins. I didn't see the damage but those who did told me that it was truly amazing what can be done to a human body by someone's fists.

'But don't you worry, Sergeant Bedwell," Keenan sounded suddenly philosophical. "Alexander Herbert will doubtless show up somewhere else in due course – possibly as a clerk in the city and living in a Mayfair apartment. I would suggest that you keep an eye on that girl of his, but I reckon you will find he has whipped her away already."

And so it had proved. Immediately after the call, Hilary had dragged Jeff Maddox out to the Beacon Community, but they had been far too late. The old red bus had gone and none of the other hippies would or could tell them where McConnel and his little family had been heading.

"Leave them alone, Sergeant," the advice came from an angular female wearing a long dress and an old fashioned bonnet. "They have their own lives to lead now. They don't need you and besides, McConnel has Ellie to look after him."

Now he was gone and Hilary sat in a comfortable two-seater settee, writing up her diary while her thoughts drifted to the strains of a Schubert symphony. She felt warm and snug in flannel pyjamas but although she had a glass of white wine at her elbow to help her sleep, her heart was breaking. Her sadness at the loss of McConnel was like a deep, physical ache in the pit of her stomach and she couldn't get rid of it.

An interruption was the last thing she needed or wanted at that moment.

"Why don't they use the ruddy phone?" She muttered crossly to herself. "They know how I hate being disturbed at home."

"Your cheeks are pink, Sergeant Bedwell."

McConnel was dressed in his old brown coat and she couldn't help noticing that for once, he wasn't wearing his matted green bobble hat. It was the first time she could recall seeing him without it, but the absence did nothing to improve his appearance. Unfettered, his tangled locks cascaded over his face and almost concealed the soft luminosity of his eyes. Eyes that for once were clear and without the cannabis film, she had grown accustomed to seeing.

Tilting his head to one side, McConnel regarded her quizzically and Hilary made a determined effort to pull herself together. She seemed to have lost all strength from her legs and her throat felt dry in spite of the wine. She couldn't just stand there though, holding the door half open with a silly grin on her face. It was hardly dignified.

"Come in McConnel." She invited in as neutral a tone as she could muster. Standing aside to let him pass, she smelled the acrid man-smell of him and was suddenly aware of her own state of undress. As he moved past, he looked deep into her eyes before reaching out with one hand and gently touching her cheek. She didn't react, but the tiny, intimate contact left her skin burning so that she had to make a determined effort not to raise her own hand to the spot where he had touched her.

"I thought you had moved on." She told him brusquely, but he ignored her and stood in the centre of her lounge, looking around him in obvious appreciation.

"What a lovely room," he murmured. "This place is definitely you, Hilary Bedwell. Schubert too;" he raised his face to listen; "you certainly have excellent taste."

Without waiting to be asked, he sat down on her settee and patted the space beside him. Moving like an automaton, Hilary did as she was bid and sat primly, her hands clasped on her knees and her body a good foot and a half from his.

McConnel looked levelly at her for a moment and there was an unfathomable expression in his eyes.

"I take it, you and your gorilla managed to pick up Joe Wemyss without any hassle?"

She started at the softly spoken question.

"Did you know that we had nick named him Thursday Joe?" She smiled at the inanity of her own question. "It caused quite a stir when we discovered that his name really was Joe. How did you manage to….?"

She paused at the sudden iceberg chill in the green eyes.

"Wemyss and I are from way back," he told her quietly. "We know each other too well for either of us to have any doubts as to what might or might not happen. In this case, I convinced him that it was up to him to clear my name. After all, I was under suspicion for his burglaries and I wasn't having that. Once he knew that I knew, he didn't really have much choice but to wait for you."

"I notice that you still trussed him up." She smiled and he raised a shaggy eyebrow.

"That was just in case he had second thoughts after I had gone, Sergeant Hilary. I've seen winded tortoises move faster than your lot in a hurry and I was worried that he might change his mind if you took too long. That would not have done at all."

"Of course not McConnel. You thought of everything, didn't you? We even had the tape recording to back things up more than a little."

"There was the tape recording," he agreed. "That was added insurance and I played it back to him before I left, just so that he would have no illusions as to the fix he was in."

The recording had let them all in on the meeting between Thursday Joe and McConnel. Although it was of little use in evidence, it had proved an effective lever in helping Wemyss to remember his past misdemeanours.

"Did you get to know him well in Northern Ireland?" She asked quietly and suddenly there was pain in his eyes.

"Johnny Keenan's been telling you things I see. I hoped he would not, but I suppose it was inevitable in the circumstances. When Maddox described the bloke who came to see you from Scotland Yard, it was pretty obvious to me who it was. Johnny is hardly the inconspicuous type, is he? I suppose it was your fault that he found out where I was?"

"I was only doing my job, McConnel. Once you were in the frame for Thursday Joe, I had to check you out and that seemed to cause a few itchy britches at The Yard. First I had some Chief Inspector from Special Branch

162

threatening me with all that is holy, then I was descended upon by your friend DI Keenan.

'He was alright though and obviously has your best interests at heart. He wants to hear from you, you know.'

McConnel shook his head abstractedly.

"No chance of that I'm afraid. I knew I had made a mistake when I let my first names slip to you in that damned café. You got under my guard there, Girl, but now you see the advantages of sticking to a single name?"

With a sudden disarming smile, he changed the subject.

"What chance do I have of enjoying a glass of your doubtless excellent wine?"

Feeling distinctly flustered by the situation, Hilary rose to comply with the request and once both their glasses were full, he offered her a silent toast over the rim of his goblet. There was a smile in his eyes and Hilary hastily resumed the conversation.

"It had to come out eventually, McConnel. You must know that? Even you couldn't remain hidden for ever."

"Maybe so: maybe not. I don't think anyone was actively looking for me any more. If I know Johnny Keenan, he would have been sitting back and waiting for me to come to notice somewhere. He must have hoped something like this would happen."

"And now it has," she said flatly. "What are you going to do?"

He half turned towards her, startled and obviously a little confused.

"What can I do, Hilary? I must just move on and be more careful in future. Avoid all blonde police sergeants for a start."

He smiled at her as he said the words, but Hilary felt a sudden ache in her heart. She did not want to lose this man.

"Why can't you go back in and become a soldier again? DI Keenan reckoned they would take you back without asking questions."

McConnel paused, obviously considering the question, then shook his head emphatically.

"No, that won't do I'm afraid. For me, those days are well and truly over. I am not going back to the endless cycle of killing, lying and violence. I did my job and I did it well, but once it started getting through to me exactly what I was doing, I pulled out and there cannot be any going back."

"Why didn't you just resign?" She was genuinely curious. "That way you would not have needed to hide."

He looked sombrely at her again and she felt herself drowning in the ever changing depths of his eyes. At that moment, she knew that McConnel could have done anything with her. Had he asked, she would have given him her body, abandoned her job and her home, even given him her life just for the chance of being with him.

But McConnel wasn't going to ask.

"It was never like that, Hilary. I couldn't just take my pension and go like an ordinary soldier. I was too useful to the army and besides, I knew far too much about our political lords and masters for them to let me go."

"What do you mean, McConnel?" She asked anxiously. "Surely you were still just a soldier, no matter how good you might have been?"

Although he was still looking at her, Hilary had the sudden feeling that McConnel was no longer aware of her presence. The green eyes seemed to be focussed in on himself and the pain of terrible memories was written plainly on his features. Slowly, but without any prompting from herself, Hilary's visitor began to talk.

The words were hesitant at first, wide apart and delivered only after painful pauses for recollection. As he warmed to the story, he seemed to regain a bit of confidence and at last, he seemed to be speaking freely. As he spoke, he held her hand and looked into her face, while she made no move to pull away. They sat close together on the small settee, their drinks forgotten and she listened to him as wives and lovers have listened to the tales of fighting men since the dawn of time.

As words, so long held back tumbled out of his system, McConnel retreated from the world around him. The warmth, comfort and feminine ambience of Hilary's flat gave way to the harsh, rain-swept pavements of Belfast, Londonderry and Crossmaglen. Her femininity and softly rounded form were swamped in memories of mangled bodies and the echoes of her gentle voice were replaced by the screaming insults of foul-mouthed harridans bawling obscenities and hurling missiles at the young men who were there to protect them. Hilary's soft blonde hair, creamy cheeks and gentle eyes were replaced in his tormented mind by the bewildered features of fresh-faced young soldiers, none of whom really knew what they were fighting and dying for.

He told her of the bad times; of young men leaking their lifeblood away for an ancient cause. He told her of the shocked faces of wives and children who witnessed the violence and were powerless to do anything about it. His voice dripped with scorn as he told her about the politicians who pontificated on the troubles without having any real idea of what they were talking about. In fact, he reserved special contempt for the politicians.

"They used the war in Northern Ireland as launching pads for their own well paid careers," he spat and his eyes were angry. "When things were not going well on the mainland, the Prime Minister or one of his henchmen would pay an official visit across the water and enjoy the fleshpots of Belfast for a day. Normal routine was disrupted and soldiers were taken from their regular duties just so that some jumped up nincompoop could posture in front of the cameras. How our political leaders love to be seen wearing flak jackets and tin hats when they know damned well there is little chance of bullets flying their way. How they love the attentions of a fawning press corps and how little any of them know about what really goes on."

McConnel shook his head again in deep disgust and Hilary wondered at the depths of his anger. "My father was one of them," he explained quietly. "He ranted and postured and did his little bit for the British political machine, but he didn't care one tuppeny jot for the pain and suffering caused by his oh-so-empty words. Like the rest of his kind, he spoke sanctimoniously of peace in Northern Ireland and was on the spot when the so-called Good Friday agreement was signed, but at the same time, he was sanctioning official gun running to other countries where war was tearing the ordinary people apart.

'He didn't see the broken bodies – none of them did. They didn't see the empty eyes and numbed horror of young lads – even children – caught up in a fight they didn't want any part of. No, as long as my esteemed parent had port and a cigar after his evening meal and a few credulous voters fawning at his feet, he was a happy man.

'He took his seat in the Lords when he retired and I'm sure he honestly believes that he did a good job for the people he was supposed to protect. The pompous, hypocritical fool – how little he really knows about life at the raw end of the political system he served throughout his life."

Obviously making a huge effort to pull his emotions together, McConnel smiled ruefully at his own outburst. Without looking at Hilary, he gently stroked the back of her hand. The gesture made her stomach tingle with pleasure and suddenly she was no longer aware of his grimy skin and filthy fingernails. He was an attractive man and she was a woman who felt quietly pleased to be allowed such a glimpse into his past, while at the same time her body reacted to being so physical a part of his present.

In a calmer voice, he told her of the funerals. The silent, hostile crowds and the grim-faced soldiers and policemen, tasked with mingling among them to monitor the situation. He told them of the swaggering, hard-eyed gunmen and his own undercover participation in a war that was not supposed to be taking place.

"Like I said, my Hilary, I was good at my job," his voice was sad, but her spirits jumped at the little endearment. "In spite of my privileged background – or perhaps because of it – I discovered that I was a natural interrogator and when necessary, an extremely efficient killer. Men did exactly what I told them to do and for those few who did not, death was the inevitable result. We could not afford to let them live."

Hilary squeezed his calloused hand in sympathy, but he seemed unaware of the gesture.

"We were called upon to kill in so many different ways and killing does enormous damage to the soul."

His voice was suddenly empty of emotion and at that moment she didn't think he was even aware of her presence. McConnel was talking for himself and to himself. The words seemed to tumble over each other in an agonised catharsis of spirit and the silently attentive witness was ignored. "Every soldier is trained to kill and accepts the fact that at some stage of his career, he will be called upon to do exactly that. At first, it all seems rather a joke and young men are always proud of their ability to fight, so it doesn't really feel real. When the reality looms closer, everyone wonders how they will react when it happens. There is no way of knowing and many young soldiers break down or leave the army rather than actually kill another man. Others enjoy it, some even appear to be born to it and regretfully I was one of those.

'For me and for a few like me, killing became a way of life. We didn't even have the luxury of hiding behind a rifle or killing from a distance. In fact, we seldom carried firearms, so we killed with knives, piano wire or our bare hands. For five long years, I lived with the frightened eyes of those who knew they were going to die, as well as my own deep fear and in the end, it all proved too much for me."

He told her about his fear; about the awful tension and strain of his undercover life. Of always having to look over his shoulder for the curious observer or murderous assassin. Of the terrifying prospect of discovery.

"I had a friend who blew his cover," his voice was infinitely sad and tears trickled slowly through his beard. "They shot him twice through each knee and in the stomach, then played macabre games on his body with cigarettes, pen knives and wire cutters. They did unspeakable things to him and the awful pity of it was that he was a strong man."

He paused and his expression was bleak.

"It took him a very long time to die."

For McConnel, that death had been the final straw. He had been the one to find Trooper Dave Robertson's body and the experience had tipped him over the brink.

"For weeks, I was quite mad," he told his pale-faced listener. "I wanted revenge and went out on my own in search of it. I killed indiscriminately and without feeling or caring. My world was one of overpowering hatred, which suited my masters, but was rapidly destroying me as a man.

'It couldn't last and one morning I decided that I had had enough, so I left."

"Just like that?" She queried with a tremulous smile.

"Just like that," his voice was flat. "It is not difficult to disappear in this allegedly civilised world and I had the ability and the contacts. Less than a year after leaving Belfast, I moved in to the Beacon and my soul began to sort itself out. I had a simple existence with Ellie and the kids, there was no more killing or deceit and perhaps I was beginning to find myself again. At any rate, the nightmares and memories faded and I almost began to enjoy life once again."

"Why didn't you go home? Why try and hide among the Beacon folk?"

He shook his head vehemently.

"They would soon have found me there, Girl. Besides, I could not have faced my father without it bringing back the horror and the memories of Ulster. I would not have been able to keep the hate from my eyes and I might even have killed him. I didn't want to do that, for all the contempt I feel for him and his kind.

'No, I was happier with the Beacon folk than ever I could have been among my own people."

"And then I came along?"

He looked into her eyes and she saw the tears brimming in his own. For a long moment, there was silence in the room and she became aware that he was holding both her hands and his face was very close to hers. The maleness of his presence seemed to dominate the pretty room and Hilary felt herself swimming in bottomless pools of limpid green.

"And then you came along Hilary Bedwell;" he agreed softly: "and everything changed again." There didn't seem to be anything more to say and when he took her in his arms, it was the most natural thing in the world for Hilary to respond to him as woman has responded to man through the ages.

EPILOGUE

Chief Inspector Bolton was smiling broadly when Hilary entered his office.

"Sit down Sergeant Bedwell," he said gently. "Fancy a cup of coffee?"

Hilary nodded dumbly. The Guv'nor had the reputation of being miserly with his favours and to be offered coffee in his office was regarded as the ultimate accolade for a junior officer. Bolton rang for his secretary.

"I have had the Chief Constable on the line this morning," he said to Hilary once the girl had taken the order and departed. "He is happy as a pig in the proverbial about the Thursday Joe result. You are in line for a commendation and that will look great on your record of service. He also asked me to convey his personal congratulations to your entire team."

Hilary felt herself blushing furiously, but wasn't sure how to react. She knew that such fulsome praise was hardly deserved, but she had promised McConnel that his part in the matter would not be mentioned to anyone.

"Joe Wemyss is my personal present to you," he had told her softly when she tried to discuss the matter and then he had kissed away her protestations.

"And Razor Wallace? Was he from you as well?"

She raised her eyebrows and he smiled secretively, but made no move to deny the fact.

The Chief inspector was still rumbling on and she forced her mind away from the memories. "One thing I have never been able to understand is why you decided to target Enderleigh Bishop on that particular Thursday." Bolton raised his eyebrows in question. "Had you been tipped off about Chummy's intentions or was it really an inspired guess? If it was then it was certainly a bloody good one. You must tell me your secret, Girl."

Hilary smiled winningly.

"As I told you at the time Sir, it was all down to feminine intuition. We women have to have some advantages, you know."

The somewhat incredulous Chief Inspector shook his head wonderingly and when the coffee arrived, they exchanged small talk for a while before Bolton brought her own particular problem back to life.

"Have you seen your tame crusty at all of late, Hilary? I gather from the grapevine that he has done a bunk?"

Struggling to keep her features impassive, Hilary reflected that she had to be in favour for Bolton to use her Christian name so often. Yet even that thought brought memories flooding back. "Why do I need Christian names?" McConnel had asked her. "I am not really a Christian and one name is surely enough for anyone."

There had been other reasons for his reticence and she knew that now, but at the time his attitude had seemed eminently reasonable. Why did anyone need more than one name? It was another example of the manner in which he had dominated her with the strength of his personality. If nobody had more than one name, she would never have known who he really was, yet at the time she had accepted his argument as being entirely logical. It was little wonder that he had been so successful in 'turning' people.

She had woken that morning to find her bed still warm from the imprint of his body. He had slipped away without saying farewell. He hadn't even left her a note and she knew with dreadful finality that she would never see him again. McConnel had dropped out of her life and although the hurt was only just beginning, she knew he had done it for her.

He might not be the ordinary, run of the mill hippy, but he was still very much a drop out from society and the police service would never stand for that. She had told him of her desire to make it right to the top in her chosen career and for that she had to keep herself above reproach. They both knew that having even a reformed hippy in her life would always be held against her, no matter how liberated the modern police service professed to be.

McConnel had understood that and so McConnel had gone his own way. It was tragic and it hurt, but in her heart, she knew that he had done the right thing.

"No Sir," she answered almost truthfully; "he seems to have disappeared completely and I don't know where he has gone."

"Good riddance too," the Chief Inspector almost growled the words. "I don't know what got into you there, Sergeant Bedwell. The man was a waste of human flesh – an oxygen thief and a low life of note, if ever there was one. His sort ought to be disposed of at birth. They are a drain on society and we don't need them."

For a moment Hilary felt her blood run hot at the senior officer's unexpected tirade, but she forced herself to relax. Bolton knew nothing of McConnel's past or his antecedents and in any case, his antipathy toward the hippies and their like was natural enough. With the trouble they so often caused and the mess they usually left behind them when they moved on, they had always been a drain on police resources and there was a natural enmity between the New Age people and the constabulary. She hadn't been too keen on them herself before she had come to know the unconventional leader of the Beacon Community. Knowing and loving McConnel as she did had changed her attitude and in the long run, it would probably make her a better police officer. Consoling herself with the thought, Hilary concentrated on what her superior officer was saying.

"We will have to do something about that lot up on the Beacon," Bolton went on. "The ones living in the cottage are probably alright, but I'll bet none of the others have permission to live there. Think of all the dirt and disease they could be spreading around the countryside. Besides, their camp is an eyesore and spoils a delightful little spot for visitors and picnickers."

Dirt and disease indeed! Hilary hugged her memories to her bosom and wondered what the guv'nor would say if he knew that his most promising sergeant has spent a whole night in the arms of the leading Beacon hippy. He would probably have a fit and order her to undergo instant decontamination in the nearest veterinary surgery. She couldn't help smiling at the thought and Bolton frowned.

"What is so funny, Young Lady? I know you had a soft spot for that toe rag, but I have far more experience of his kind than you do. If only the politicians would give us a bit of support, we could get rid of them all, but our lords and masters are a spineless lot. They sit on their arses in posh offices and make decisions that cause difficulties for everyone else, then congratulate themselves on doing a grand job. Most of them need to get out on the ground and see the problems for themselves, but they wouldn't think of getting their smart shoes dirty."

Hilary smiled again, although she made sure that it was only to herself. The burly officer in charge was echoing the sentiments of the man he so despised and she was tempted to tell him so, but restrained herself with difficulty. It seemed that in so many ways, all men were alike and she couldn't help chuckling at the thought. As she left the Chief Inspector's office, he called her back. "Oh Sergeant Bedwell;" she turned and he smiled; "the ACC has changed his mind about your application to join the Armed Response Team. It seems that you are good enough after all and your first training day is next Friday."

For a moment, anger and the memory of McConnel's stories about guns in Northern Ireland tempted Hilary to withdraw her application, but she contented herself with her prettiest smile.

"Thank you Sir," she said sweetly and left the room.

After all, a small Cotswold farming town was a long way from Belfast and she wanted to get on.

***

As the sun went down, Sergeant Hilary Bedwell stood on the very pinnacle of Swanwick Beacon. Around her the countryside was silent at the gradual disappearance of another day, while far below her vantage point, the lights of the town twinkled into life.

Hilary had finished work for the day and was in civilian clothes. She had driven alone up to the Beacon and having parked her car in a clearing, set off on a walk through the rapidly darkening woods. She wasn't quite sure why she was doing it, but it was with no great surprise that she found herself looking down on the little grey cottage and the dilapidated wooden buildings that hid behind it. She had stood in this same spot every almost every evening in the month or more since she had last seen McConnel. Even to herself, it seemed an awfully masochistic thing to do.

The hurt of his leaving had seemed almost too much to bear for a while and even now, it lingered on, but she had found herself with a great deal of work to distract her. The Thursday Joe case had led to an enormous amount of paperwork and there were files on Razor Wallace and Abie Whitehead to prepare for Court. Alison Mayberry had been found in Glasgow and there had been other cases to keep her busy. As the days went by, McConnel's memory lost its capacity to hurt her quite so intensely.

Turning away from the survey beacon, Hilary wandered back into the trees. She had come to enjoy her solitary evening vigils and understood how the peaceful ambience of the Beacon had so appealed to McConnel. Somehow, knowing that he too had sat up there so often made him seem closer to her and enabled her to get over her disappointment at his going.

It was dark in the woods, but after so many such walks, she knew her way around and had no difficulty in picking out the path that led to her car. A huge oak tree caught her eye and as she was in no particular hurry, she moved across to sit at its base and relax with her memories for a little longer. Leaning back against the gnarled old trunk, Hilary indulged herself by reliving every moment of that wonderful night.

She smiled as she felt McConnel's hard hands roaming across her body and lingering on the pink-tipped mounds of her breasts. She moved her shoulders in whispered delight as his lips moved softly across her skin. The secret place between her legs tingled at the memory of his caresses and for a long, blissful moment, Sergeant Hilary Bedwell was once again, a young and beautiful woman, alone with the man she adored.

But it was too good to last and with a sigh of nostalgic regret, Hilary rose to her feet. A huge, orange moon was rising over the hills and in its ethereal light, she spotted a darker shadow on the ground nearby. Moving across, she picked it up and even in the pale light, she had no difficulty in recognising the green, woollen bobble hat he had always worn.

With a grin of pure delight, she rubbed the smelly little garment against her cheek and savoured its damp mustiness in her nostrils. Whatever else happened, she would have one tiny piece of McConnel to remember him by and she tucked the dreadful hat into the waistband of her skirt. Setting off down the hill once more, the spring was back in her step and her spirits were lightened by the unexpected connection with the man she loved.

From the darkness of the trees, a pair of deep green eyes watched her go and the man, known only as McConnel was also smiling as he moved away in the opposite direction.

THE END

Other books by David Lemon

Ivory Madness: The College Press 1983

Africa's Inland Sea: Modus Press 1987

Kariba Adventure: The College Press 1988

Rhino: Puffin Books 1989

Man Eater: Viking Books 1990

Hobo Rows Kariba: African Publishing Group 1997

Killer Cat: The College Press 1998

Never Quite a Soldier: Albida Books 2000

Never Quite a Soldier: Galago Books 2006 **(South African edition)**

Blood Sweat and Lions: Grosvenor House Publishing 2008

Two Wheels and a Tokoloshe: Grosvenor House Publishing 2008

Hobo: Grosvenor House Publishing 2009

Soldier No More: Grosvenor House Publishing 2011

Cowbells Down the Zambezi: Grosvenor House Publishing 2013

The Poacher: Socciones Editoria Digitale 2016

In Livingstone's Footsteps: Socciones Editoria Digitale 2016

27165688R00106

Printed in Poland
by Amazon Fulfillment
Poland Sp. z o.o., Wrocław